Praise for *Aesthetica*

"A tragic tale about clout-chasing your way off a cliff in the Instagram era." —*New York Magazine*'s **The Cut**

"*Aesthetica* is not only timely, it's also necessary reading." —*The Observer*

"A novel for anyone who exist wrestled with the dissonance b online and the body they inhab probing account of fame and a gaze that creates the culture we live within. —*Los Angeles Review of Books*

"[A] twisted deep dive into the sordid nature of social media . . . *Aesthetica* is a brutal novel that forces you to look in the mirror before breaking it and using the shards to cut you open." —**Buzzfeed**

"Rowbottom explores the future of our relationship with social media with raw honesty, nuance, and compassion." —**BookRiot**

"[Examines]—and occasionally eviscerates—everything from social media consumption, to vanity, feminism, the city of Los Angeles and beyond." —*The Hollywood Reporter*

"Allie's writing is a light to follow in the dark, illuminating those human realities we often wish would stay hidden, but deep down, if we're open enough, are grateful to have seen all the same." —**Dantiel W. Moniz, author of *Milk Blood Heat***

"*Aesthetica* is the best book about influencers I've ever read and the only book about the internet that doesn't make the author sound like a thousand-year-old vampire."

—Caroline Calloway

"Propulsive, poetic, and addictive as hell, *Aesthetica* is a wholly original look not only into the world of social media influencers, but into the lives beyond the squares that are devastatingly rich in heart, depth, and ultimately, redemption. Allie Rowbottom writes like a wizard."

—Chelsea Bieker, author of *Godshot* and *Heartbroke*

"A gothic twist on the contemporary woman's life. Immersive, wicked, and so much fun. Allie Rowbottom is the only writer that should be writing on this era of Instagram and Influencers." —Marlowe Granados, author of *Happy Hour*

"There's nothing supernatural afoot in *Aesthetica*, but when Anna slurs 'I'm a star' while high on Percocet, staring at her phone, proud of her own worst impulses, it's as terrifying as any tale of a woman in thrall to wicked powers." —*Wired*

"Complex and deeply engaging ... A scorching commentary on society's blindness toward female pain. Fans of Mary Gaitskill's work and *Black Mirror* will flock to this pitch-perfect novel." —*Publishers Weekly*, **Starred Review**

"Rowbottom wades through dueling waves of feminism, affectionate and critical of both second- and post-wave ideologies ... There is no clear moral at the end *Aesthetica*, no satisfactory conclusion, no unified theory of implants, no winner in a culture war." —*BOMB* Magazine

AESTHETICA

ALLIE ROWBOTTOM

SOHO

Published by
Soho Press, Inc.
227 W 17th Street
New York, NY 10011

Library of Congress Cataloging-in-Publication Data

Names: Rowbottom, Allie, author.
Title: Aesthetica / Allie Rowbottom.
Description: New York, NY : Soho, [2022]
Identifiers: LCCN 2022023012

ISBN 978-1-64129-532-1
eISBN 978-1-64129-401-0

Subjects: LCGFT: Novels.
Classification: LCC PS3618.O87258 A66 2022 | DDC 813/.6—dc23/eng/20220525
LC record available at https://lccn.loc.gov/2022023012

Interior design by Janine Agro, Soho Press, Inc.

Printed in the United States of America

10 9 8 7 6 5 4 3 2 1

"Everyone says you were beautiful when you were young, but I want to tell you I think you're more beautiful now than then. Rather than your face as a young woman, I prefer your face as it is now. Ravaged."

—Marguerite Duras, *The Lover*

"I look at myself as an art project, and I'll create whatever I want until I want to stop."

—Erika Jayne

PART ONE

1.

I am on my phone, of course I am. But the screams start, sudden as the sound of my own name. I look up. It's only a group of girls, huddled by the hot tub. They lift arms, devices, as if in prayer; they still themselves before the lens, a ritual. Three flashes and again, they shriek, each *omg* another post, another like, another love. They are alive in their bodies, together in their bodies; I feel their oneness inside me, like hunger.

The plate before me is empty, though. Just the rind of a bacon cheeseburger to remind me what I ate. On this white daybed. In my bikini, which is also white. Ketchup dripped down my chin, landed on my breasts, smatterings of B-movie blood I wipe with my whole hand, lick clean. I lie back, body bare and distended. I'm satiated, but the feeling always passes and the meal was freighted, like everything today, with the possibility that it might be my last.

I fish a bottle from my black and white striped bag, snap the cap, swallow a pill with spit. I suck a vape to erase the chemical taste, blow cones of watermelon smoke toward the girls. They're cute, but each one needs a tweak to achieve true beauty. *Rhinoplasty*, I diagnose when I look at one. *Brow lift*, I silently suggest for another. *Buccal fat pad removal.*

In the big pool, a woman my age props her elbows on an inflatable raft. Nearby, a child, chubby with preadolescence, slumps sidesaddle on a foam noodle. Clearly they are together, clearly they are one, both redheaded and freckled, pear-shaped bodies waved as blown glass beneath the water. The mother says something and the child doesn't answer, just stares at the hot tub, the girls. When I was young like her, I wanted nothing more than to emerge. Out into the seen world, the world of teenagers I saw on TV, girls I followed on Instagram. Girls who siphoned attention, desire, love, with reckless ease. Girls tweaked into fantasies I thought were real.

"Isabelle," the mother says. The number eleven between her eyebrows is so deep it threatens permanence. I touch my skin like I'm checking it's still there. My forehead remains, pulled tight as a starched sheet and I want, for a moment, to wrinkle it. I want to become the other woman. A mother, a daughter, a purer version of myself; I want to become them all.

I swallow to melt the pill further down my throat. I suck the vape. Isabelle lifts herself from the pool. Water pulls at her swimsuit. She pads to a set of lounge chairs, wraps herself in a terry cloth robe. It dwarfs her. I lift my phone, pinch the screen of space between us, zoom in to see her better. She turns to face me and I press the shutter, smile. She looks away. Scared, maybe.

Wrapped in her towel, the mother stands, gathers her bag,

ready to leave. Isabelle stands next and I stand too, so fast the world spots with blue. I blink through the blur, rush to gather my things. My phone, my bag, my flip-flops, kicked carelessly beneath the daybed. I have to squat to extract them. When I rise, I look for the woman and the girl. But my gaze lands only on a man, watching me from a nearby cabana. He's older, sixties-ish, with his Kindle and iced tea, his Teva sandals and cargo shorts. His mirrored aviators in which I swear I see myself, gut unfurled, the burger inside adding to the paunch. I suck in for a moment. Then breathe out, let myself expand, let fat push up against scar tissue and skin, let the man look. I slip my feet into my sandals, one quick scuff, then another, and follow the wet footprints left by the woman and the girl; I follow the path they took away from me.

2.

Summer, 2017. Fifteen years in the past, the day I'd say my story starts, the start of a transformation I'm only now completing. Some chain wax center in West Hollowood and my half-naked body reclined on a sheet of butcher paper. Speakers on the ceiling spewed a pop song about fire and love. I looked up at panels of fluorescent light, a poster of a woman at a nice restaurant. Her hands were folded over the white napkin in her lap; her skin shone, concave and hairless; a steamed lobster on the table stared up at her, scarlet carapace still unbroken.

"Knees to chest," the waxist said. She had an accented, angular voice. I held my shins as she slathered steaming blue to my labia, the insides of my ass cheeks. The room was cold, the hot wax a comfort. "Just like a virgin," she said and patted before she pulled.

Pain flashed where the hair had been. A screaming hole I closed my eyes to slip inside. I wanted it. A womanly ritual, the hurting, my ability to stand it. One I might complain about with girlfriends, like period cramps, all of us in on the same unspoken joke, the suffering required by a certain sort of body.

I thought of my mother, the vacation we took from Houston to LA two summers before. Orange light in our Hollywood hotel room and her body, squatting and squirming from the bathroom in a new cerulean one-piece. "Five decades of bathing suits and I still can't figure out where everything's supposed to go," she said. "What do you think?" She turned a circle, cocked a hip, the blue suit shone and the waxist wrenched the final strip, returning me to the room.

"Baby," the waxist said, "you like?" I opened my eyes and craned my neck to see a swath of pubic hair, smaller than a thumbprint. It stunned me, my own skin, infantile and pink; the coarse brown "landing strip" seemed somehow indecisive.

"Maybe just take it all?" I said. The waxist nodded, returned to her pot, globbed blue over the remainder. She fanned, then pulled. "What you think now?"

"What do you think?" my mother had repeated that night in Hollywood, when it was just us two in the orange light, assessing her new bathing suit. And I had been a mean girl.

"Uh, you need a wax," I said, trying out a new voice.

Her face flushed. "Well, obviously," she said. I buried myself in my phone. She disappeared into the bathroom, emerged in a towel. Later, while brushing my teeth, I spotted curlicued black hairs crowding the blades of her razor like weeds pushing through the shutters of a boarded-up house and felt angry in a way that made me want to be even meaner. I was harsh but she was clueless. How was she still such a little girl? Why was it my job to explain bikini lines and makeup application, lessons of womanhood her own mother died too young to impart? I learned them from YouTube, Instagram, and though my mother said she wanted instruction too, she never stuck with the rituals I prescribed. Contouring and gua sha massage, retinol and ten-step serum routines, all abandoned, as if she thought learning to care for herself would rob her own mom of the chance to rise from the dead and teach her.

"Baby?" The waxist wanted answers.

"Okay," I said.

She puffed cold powder onto my crotch. "Baby," she said, "You go now."

I dressed, bare skin behind my clothes like a secret, safe with me, a pulled together girl, all the mess shorn off. A girl wise enough to identify the mess in the first place, and to fix it. I tipped using a formula my mother taught me (move the decimal point, then double it), called a car and walked out into Los Angeles. Ash on the air, and fire.

MY LYFT DRIVER was a man who spoke with fear about his teenage daughter. "Six thousand dollars to get her on drill team," he said. "But she has to maintain a 4.0. Then she can do what she wants."

"Smart," I said.

"What do you do?" he asked.

I didn't have an answer. I had only been in Los Angeles two weeks, only been a high school graduate for six. No father cared what I did or didn't do; mine had always been absent.

Rich and old, he'd left by my third birthday. But in a way, he'd given me a gift, freedom, by abandoning me. Because here I was, hustling harder for what I'd lost.

"I'm a freshman at USC," I told the driver, a lie in the shape of what I thought he wanted to hear. We pulled up to my Airbnb.

"Be safe out there, baby," he said. I thanked him, got out, rolled my eyes. As if he knew what was safe for girls. As if his own daughter wasn't miserable most likely, forced onto the drill team, so lame.

THE AIRBNB WAS a room in a bungalow off Robertson, shared with three other girls—community theater kids turned Hollywood waitstaff, auditioning endlessly, whining about flakey agents and acting coaches. Girls with next to no internet presence, who wanted a different sort of stardom, a different screen. When I suggested they build platforms, use Instagram to get noticed, they thanked me, but laughed a little, snarky, like they thought social media was superficial, uncreative, a crutch. So almost as soon as I moved in, I stopped talking to them. At night, they sat around the communal kitchen table running lines, projecting and enunciating like they were already on stage. To escape them, I walked. Beyond the smoke, the air smelled of flowers. Red bougainvillea draped over balconies and looked, in the fading light, like entrails, touched with blue. I took photos for my feed, captured the LA light, the Spanish-style mansions, winding wrought iron, ocean on the air, which cooled at night to a deep desert chill I'd never felt before. All of it was so new, so utterly unlike Houston, my mother, the stale and humid library where she worked, the chronic complaints she made about her body—its size and shape and ailments—always searching for something to cure. I turned the camera to my face and spoke as I walked. "Gonna be a big staaaah," I said and smooched the lens.

I had reason to believe I could touch stardom, and the money that came with it, as a model on Instagram. This is what I'd told my mother, how I'd sold her on my move to LA. Instagram was a business opportunity, a new frontier for entrepreneurial youths like me, youths with initiative. College stifled that sort of thing and I had read online that even rich kids were taking gap years to experience the real world. I had read that student debt was shackling my generation, condemning us to the same hardship I watched my mother weather, month by month, a running list of questions: which bills needed paying, which she could put off, what could she forego. Travel, therapy, dental work. The real world, shrunken by lack. But technology was wide open. It was where the money was. Influencers with one hundred thousand followers earned a thousand dollars a post, easy. Two hundred thousand followers equaled paid vacations to five-star resorts. Almost foolish, to want to do anything else.

I was fourteen when I received a phone of my own, but I already knew how to use it. The first thing I did was save Leah's number under the contact "BEST FRIEND FOREVER." My mother's I saved as "Mommy," which I still sometimes called her. The second thing I did was start an Instagram account, gather followers with hashtags and selfies that accentuated my youth, the teeth that took up half my face when I smiled.

My mother said my smile belonged to the grandmother who'd died before my birth. "You look so like her," she would say and gesture at framed photographs, old black and white images of the beautiful mother she'd lost too soon. It was a source of pride for my mom, to have produced a child to carry on the legacy of her own mom's bright smile. But she was wrong. I was prettier than my grandmother ever was. I was special, destined to transcend the small lives of the women who came before me; I was deserving of DMs from Instagram scouts, brand offers to "collab."

The only message I replied to, spring of my junior year of high school, had all the markings of a scam. It was, instead, a fluke, a job modeling festival wear for a brand called Hippy Baby, based in Austin, a job for a girl with management, a comp card and portfolio. But someone had fallen through, someone had said *rush*, some scout plucked me off Instagram and said I had a "trademark smile," all teeth. I was seventeen, barely licensed. But I drove my mother's car the whole way, I-10 to I-71, three hours through wildflower fields to a loft downtown, a photographer named Eric, his nameless assistant, who was a girl my age. They rearranged my body like furniture, both frustrated that I was so unpracticed. "Where do I change?" I asked after the first outfit was shot and they said, "Wherever," like I should know. In the room's middle, I bent to pull up bikini bottoms, or to drop them, and imagined my asshole puckering in the air conditioned cold, how they would see it too. If they did, they didn't say. They didn't care about my asshole, just my ass itself, just the outside. "You've got a butt," Eric told me when he finished shooting. "But you've got a gut, too." He said nothing of my smile. "I'm keto and I love it," his assistant said. She was friendlier once the work was done. And yet I left alone and hungry, just the photographer's voice in my head, the word *gut*, repeating.

When the pictures posted I catapulted from 6,000 to 20,000 Instagram follows, earned $4,000. So much growth, so quickly. Like the solution to an ailment I hadn't known I suffered, a power I'd known was possible, but hadn't anticipated would be easy to claim. So easy, the number of dollars in my account, the number of people at my fingertips, all of them wanting, waiting for solutions I might offer, products I might sell, power I might promise. When I hit 20,000 I screamed and jumped and took a selfie, trademark smiling, proving to myself how happy I was. But really, I was thinking of what more I could make for myself, what more I could make for my mother, now that I was backed by a number that would continue to grow if I worked at it, leveraged my number for a bigger, better number. Leverage was how empires were built, the walls of a well-made house high and thick and every bill paid on time, everyone inside healthy and safe. I subscribed to *Business Insider*, spent hours reading beyond their paywall. I learned that persistence is an essential quality of successful entrepreneurs. *Gut*, I thought when I took selfies. *Keto*, I whispered when I opened the fridge. It felt like a promise Los Angeles could help me keep and I begged my mother for a trip. Finally, when summer came— my seventeenth, her forty-eighth—she agreed. We flew from Houston to Los Angeles for Star Tours, studio tours, the Hollywood Sign. We stayed three nights, walked for three days up and down Sunset Boulevard, Melrose Boulevard, Hollywood Boulevard, in and out of amusement parks: Universal Studios, California Adventure, and the newly opened Fairy Tale Land, our favorite. Afterward, I imagined graduating high school and returning to LA. And now here I was, returned.

LATE NIGHTS IN the Airbnb, once my housemates went quiet, I turned on every lamp in my room, set up my ring light and tripod, which was cheap and plastic. I arranged its spider legs tenderly, like a girl with a doll, then took off all my clothes and experimented with angles that suggested, but did not show, my naked body. *Gut. Keto.* Facetune. Photoshop, which I'd learned in an afterschool class my freshman year of high school. At the time, I used Instagram filters, but that was all. At the time, it sort of outraged me, how people were Photoshopping their content in secret. So even as I learned to alter my images, I told myself I'd use my power carefully. The class progressed, and I got into searching for Instagram versus reality accounts that placed celebrities' and influencers' untouched photos and unpaid paparazzi candids next to the edited images they posted on their accounts: realistic waists and jaws slimmed down and snatched, cellulite painted over, passed off as real. Yes, it *outraged* me to see how they'd lied. It entranced me, what they truly looked like versus what they shared. "There should be a law against this," I said at first, sitting on my mom's couch, hunched, scrolling. She stood over my shoulder, hands shoved into the pouch of her giant hoodie, and squinted at the screen. "Absolutely," she said, then something about teen depression, on the rise since Facebook, Instagram, Snapchat started promoting impossible ideals. "Texas State has a good law program," she said and wandered into the kitchen. I heard cabinets open, close. She wanted me to do a year at Houston Community College, then transfer. "Maybe you'll grow up and write that law."

Maybe. But the longer I looked, the more I wondered if image alteration might actually be empowering. For women, so often robbed of agency, was there some freedom in controlling how the world saw our bodies, consumed our bodies? My final project for that Photoshop course was my own image, edited every which way. A smile where there'd been a frown. Smooth skin where there'd been acne scars. Absence where there'd been fat and flesh. Fat and flesh where there'd been absence. Yeah, it was empowering to decide which version I preferred.

NOW, IN LOS Angeles, I added footage of my nightly walk to an edited version of my body—legs angled to hide my hairless bush, arms shaved down and wrapped around myself, showing a small side of breast; my face glossed and contoured and just a glint of brighter, whiter teeth—and tagged the post "Hollywood," and shared it. And slept. In the late morning, I woke, reached right for my phone. Sometime in the night, a verified Instagram user had DMed me. His name was Jake Alton and he liked my account. Would I want to meet? The message read like it was dashed off. Like maybe Jake Alton wrote a lot of messages like it. I put my hand over my mouth. "*Omg*," I yelled through the muffle. I went to Jake's grid and scrolled: Jake Alton riding a surfboard; Jake Alton paragliding, cave jumping, BMX bike riding; Jake Alton with this or that recognizable, powerful man. I scrolled back to the top: "Jake Alton, content creator, manager, *a simple man with complex tastes*," and a blue check mark, 1.1 million followers. Jake Alton, a simple, complex, careful algorithm, worth so many followers, so much love.

The curtains in my room were thin. The sun cut through them the way it cut the morning marine layer, the smoke and evening smog: like a blade. I rolled onto my back, held my phone high as I replied to Jake. Yes, I would love to meet a star like him. Yes, I used the word love. I used the word star.

3.

The pool is shaped like a heart, the hotel like a castle. It's close to Warner Bros, the Burbank airport and LA's lesser theme parks. I booked it because I thought I'd feel safe here. And the hotels in Beverly Hills are too expensive. In the lobby of this one: a chandelier made of fake antlers, a display case of three-hundred-dollar crystal crowns, two white and pink thrones, for selfies. "Boutique," I read online before I booked. But everything feels dated.

I hurry to the elevator bank, look around, punch the up button too hard. Somewhere between here and the pool I lost the woman and the girl. Without them, all I want is the safety of my own room, solitary and dark. The doors ding open, shut, open again, on a floor that feels deserted, coated in a deep purple light cast by tinted lamps, absorbed by purple carpet. The hallway is intolerably long, lined with door after door of possible disappearances. I imagine my body dragged across the threshold, swallowed. But maybe this is what I want, a violent disappearance. I breathe for a count of three to get my nerve up, then speed walk to my room with my key card out and ready. Inside, I turn every lock, catch my breath, taste mildew. Even the mold is air conditioned, the whole room so cold the carpet's damp, or feels like it. The furnishings are ornately carved, like a princess's, the way I remember Fairy Tale Land, everything medieval, but also plastic, worlds like pages out of a child's bath-time book, whimsical and water-resistant.

The bathroom fan rattles. I drop my bikini bottoms, unlace my top, let it fall, then glance at the mirror, always startled by what I see. Dimples, ripples, reminders of masks and knives and wrist ties. A certain willful proximity to death itself. I give myself a conspiratorial look, the kind of look you give a friend who asks how you are when obviously you're shitty. And shut the light.

In the bedroom, I bend to the mini fridge, remove a bottle of wine. My own, not the twenty-dollar, two hundred milliliter the hotel provides. I came prepared. My wine bottle, my vape pen, nineteen bars of Xanax, thirteen Ambien, fifty Vicodin. And six gel caps, prefilled with magic mushrooms, a drug I've never tried. My dealer threw them in with my last order. "Nature's medicine," he said. I think he's worried about me.

The screw cap snaps. The bottle pours. My glass is paper, made for coffee. I set it on the bedside table, wrap myself in a robe and climb into bed, turn on the TV. The word "breaking" runs on a reel across the bottom of the screen. Twenty-four-hour news, the same story that's been told for days. A powerful man, his desire, his violence, the world's permissiveness.

There's an orange bottle next to the wine. I open it, shake

a circle into my palm, pale pink as a contraceptive. I swallow, pick up the remote, scroll sound and color, pause on a home improvement network. A powder blond couple shops for a starter house in North Carolina. They look like real people, with eye bags and muffin tops. But nothing is what it looks like; the show is staged. Still, I watch for a while, top off my glass, drink. Mineral, dank notes of pear and flower. "Dream house," the woman says. "Man cave," says the man.

From the bedside table, my phone pings and I reach for it, find its glassy face stacked with notifications. Instagram DMs mostly: sex bots, scam bots and a reporter for *Vanity Fair* who writes to me often, asking for my story about a man from my past. I swipe away, open my texts, touch the one unread blue dot. "Reminder: your facial procedure at The Aesthetica Center is tomorrow, check in at 6 A.M., reply YES to confirm."

"YES" I type, and send. The phone makes the sound of zipping and a bot responds, thanking me. I've waited months to be here, on the verge of the appointment I just confirmed. That I would cancel now, that I even could, plucks a dreaded cord behind my sternum. Because I have to go through with it. This is my chance. I won't have another one.

I close the phone, put it face down on my chest and find the remote, pump the volume to drown out my thoughts. One episode ends, a new one begins. A mother and daughter want to flip a house together. Like magic, I watch them turn a total gut-job into a pristine starter home, open concept, with subway tile bathrooms. Fragments of my mother's voice filter in: *God grant me the serenity to accept the things I cannot change. Be the change you want to see. Revise the negative self-talk.*

I pick up the phone again, open my photos and examine the picture I took of the girl at the hotel pool, the anxious mother in her background. Frizzy hair and foam noodles. Nothing is what it looks like. Their sameness and skin, my mother's and mine. Seventeen years ago in Fairy Tale Land, her arm around my waist in front of *Fairy Godmother's Magic Wand Shop.*

"Put your tongue behind your teeth when you smile," I told her. "And one leg in front of the other." We posed. The camera flashed. The Xanax meets the Vicodin and together they spread out inside me. The woman and girl walk the rooms of their renovated tract house. I dream, as I often do, of meals I didn't mean to eat, drugs I didn't mean to swallow, faceless men I didn't want to fuck. Even in sleep, I open my mouth, and scream.

4.

I met Jake Alton for the first time at a club in downtown LA. Password protected, private, the perfect place to discuss my future, he said. I carried my phone, debit card and license in a cheap silver clutch that matched my dress, also metallic, also cheap, loose everywhere but my ass and nipples. They tented the fabric like bones.

"You sure, hon?" the driver said when he dropped me off. Around us: broken buildings, streetlights either dead or flickering on their way. I wasn't sure and felt uneasy for a moment. But successful entrepreneurs say yes to any potential opportunity. And sometimes that's uncomfortable. I pointed to a line of people hunched outside a green metal door. "I think that's me," I said.

Music roared behind the door. I stood near the line, but not in it, and texted Jake, "Here." Thumb on the screen, I waited, worrying about my age, the date on my license, the fake ID I didn't have. I had just turned nineteen and my body still looked like a girl's body. Which Jake said wouldn't be a problem.

Minutes passed and no response. I felt watched by the

people in line, judged, like they might assume I thought myself better than them, standing apart as I was. I folded one arm over my chest and scrolled my phone, considering how to appear casual, chill, considering what TV show, movie, Instagram feed I could draw from to appear casual, chill. Anything but awkward or worse, anxious; anxiety, to me, was my mother's purview.

"You're pushing me away," she had started to complain after our trip to Los Angeles, after the Hippy Baby pictures posted, as I prepared to move for good. At first, I reassured her with lengthy descriptions of my business plan (gain followers, get sponsors, make money), and promises to text her every day. But the last time she said it—*you're pushing me away*—I didn't look up from my phone. She snapped her fingers at the space between my face and the screen. "Anna," she yelled.

"You simply can't stand that I'm not like you," I told her, my voice matter of fact, cold.

ALONE AND JACKETLESS in the desert night, I shivered. The line was getting longer. Still scrolling, I walked to the end of it and took my place behind a group of girls, two guys in tow. They all turned to look at me, then back to each other, and the silver dress, which at home in the small and streaky bathroom mirror had looked expensive, felt cheap the way I knew it was. I checked my phone for Jake again, saw nothing and thought of catfishers, scammers, stories of stupid girls, too eager to be wanted, too easily punished for it. But

then, a buzzing. A blue bubble and in it, Jake's name. "Don't
get in line," he wrote and washed me in relief. I saw him appear
at the door, saw him from beyond all those waiting bodies. He
held a hand up high and waved me to where he was. I unfolded
my arms, put my phone in my clutch, left the line, and went
to him.

He wore a suit, the collar of his dress shirt unbuttoned,
prayer beads on his wrists and laced loose around his throat.
"You look hot," he said and leaned in to kiss my cheeks.
The feeling—his skin against mine—thrilled me, scared me,
thrilled me again. I tried to see his face, but all I saw were
flashes: fabric and skin. I had seen Jake's account, though, the
pictures of Jake's face: chiseled cheekbones and his trademark
tousled hair, worn most often in a bun atop his head. He was
hot in a manufactured way. Soon I would be too. But always, I
wanted to see him without a filter; for our entire time together,
I would wonder what he looked like completely naked.

The bouncer waved us in, underhanded, his eyes fixed on
the line I'd left. Jake took my hand and his palm was clammy. I
moved closer, close enough to eke heat, close enough to smell
his Acqua Di Giò, which all the boys in my high school had
worn. Jake was twenty-nine but he reeked "fresh aromatic"
like an eighteen-year-old, familiar, unthreatening. He led me
down a narrow hallway, a dark canal that opened into vampiric
light, house music and beautiful bodies arrayed in patterns that
seemed ornamental, everyone with wet, parted lips and drinks
in their hands. Like something from a movie, something I

hadn't believed existed in real life. But I had wanted it to be real, had surrendered my self-limiting beliefs, and now here it was, real. Girls on Instagram called this *manifestation*. Entrepreneurial gurus like Tony Robbins and Pat Flynn called it *creating one's own reality*. The music swelled. Strobes timed to match it split the dark. So I could still see Jake's eyes when he turned to face me, pewter blue contact lenses, too bright to be real, obviously fake. And almost bold because of it. But also basic, dated, especially next to the beads, the cologne. Though he didn't seem to know it. I knew the truth and Jake did not and this gave me power.

Mine was, "the fickle power of teenage girlhood," a temporary currency, according to my mother. Objectifying myself could never make me happy, she said, though she was wrong. Her version of feminism was outdated, too rigid to work in the real, digital world where I was in control of my body, my content, and smart to leverage the short blush of my youth for what was permanent and sure: power like Jake's, his power to sign and promote me, his power not to. His was a power shored up by money and other men's power. His was the power of choice, the power to leave and not be left. Which was what I wanted. To transcend my mother's fate, and mine. To make more of our abandonment, my father's leaving. I wanted to turn the story around and choose how I spent my time, made my money, presented my body. I wanted the power that came with certainty, what was real, what was illusion. I wasn't sure there was a difference, wasn't sure there should be.

Jake led me through the club, walking with a languid gait, his shoulders rolled back so that his heart looked open and imperiled. We sat at a sticky banquette. There was a bucket on the table before us, champagne on ice, clean flutes on a tray. He poured me one, tipping the glass to stanch the foam, graceful in how he held the stem, which felt breakable in my hand, dangerous. I tried to look comfortable. Jake sat back and sipped, so I did also. We checked our phones, turned them face down, checked again, sipped again. A waitress brought tiny strawberries on a platter and Jake plopped one into my champagne. It fizzed at the bottom until I swallowed it whole and poured myself another glass. Jake talked about his latest trip, to Peru, where he had done Ayahuasca and "seen the point of it all."

"I'm telling you," he said, "something clicked in my brain, like a new neural pathway. Like, before I would have looked at you and seen your hair, you skin, your smile, your eyes, your whole *ascetic*."

"Aesthetic," I said.

"Anyway, now I see your soul, and the fucking crazy thing is, it's my soul too."

We were, Jake said, as all humans and animals and plants and life forms were, part of the same consciousness, divided at birth into independent bodies. He touched his collarbones, his pecs. He tapped his phone and was silent for a beat, checking. He turned back to me, touched my leg.

"It's all an illusion," he said, and I knew he was making a

commitment, telling me this mindset informed his managerial skills, which he called "conscious" and "nurturing."

I was humoring him when I nodded, smiled, told him he was right. I was playing a part to get to his power, measuring every move I made against moves I'd seen other desirable women—girls—make: the way Daul Kim leaned forward for the camera, swan-necked and skinny-armed; the way Kendall Jenner touched her fingers to the tip of her shoulders, turned a cheek, and glowered. My body was the result of those other women's bodies, and now the club itself, which had closed around me and altered what power meant to me, what it looked like, and who I was willing to become, to make power my own. This was experience, adulting, trying on roles, creating my own reality. A reality in which Jake, who had at first seemed corny and canned, was starting to glow, a twilit vampire, his skin like a little girl's fantasy of paternal love, always beaming.

"Let's get out of here," he said and stood, pulled me up with him. I followed him back through the crowd, back down the dark canal and into a night that was brighter now, a sort of daylight.

ON THE CURB, Jake called an Uber with one hand and brushed my ass with the other, casual. I checked my Instagram and leaned toward the cup of his palm. My last post, the picture of my nearly naked body, the bougainvillea from my walk, had earned 627 likes, twenty comments. I'd received seven DMs since Jake's, monosyllabic messages from gamer guys and faceless bots and old men whose grids were stacked with expensive cars. "Hey," they wrote and "question . . ." and "pretty" and "love your page." I tapped each one and hearts rose up.

A bright blue BMW arrived. Jake held the door. I tucked my phone into my clutch and we lowered in.

"You're going to the Rainbow Room, yeah?" The driver wore sunglasses despite the night.

Jake said, "Yeah, bro," and put a hand on my thigh. I looked to the front seat, the driver's invisible eyes. Jake's hand inched higher. Blood beat from my knees to my crotch and I turned to face him. The car pulled to a stop. He took his hand away.

Inside the Rainbow Room, there was a fireplace, a bar. "A lot of famous rockers hang out here," Jake said. In booths aging men with long gray hair huddled, the air above them ringed in smoke. Like the people in wolf costumes who roamed Fairy Tale Land and waited tables at *Red Riding Hood's Roadhouse*, where my mother had ordered cheap wine for us both. It arrived in shapely plastic flagons, an adult beverage we both knew I was too young to drink. But I drank it anyway, and she let me, a sly smile on her face as the room warmed and we both began to giggle.

"I love it here," I said to Jake. It was the right thing to say.

"You love it," he said and asked if he could kiss me. I told him yes. His mouth was like Dentyne Ice, mezcal. Like putting myself in front of the camera, like thousands of likes piling up, hundreds of comments—

@inesbnld: 😑😑😑

@delphinegendron: Beautiful 😍🖤

@Love_Certified: Amazing! 🐬

@Under_the_influence_reality: Iconic!!🖤

@sebahormazabal: 👍👌

@mr.nearlynice: Nice

@maeda346: So nice

@cameron_paul: Sweet and pretty :)

@wells_spring_viiana: eu não pego ninguém mesmo, não vai fazer falta kkkkkk

@Dr_6689: You're so beautiful

@kellykimmyjames: 👍👌🖤🖤🖤🖤🖤🖤

@storevast: Astonishing

—All of them confirming that I was right, had played the game right. I was the best, most beautiful, sweet and pretty, astonishing and iconic. A victory, that I could be all these things when my mother could not. And a sign of how clueless she was about where power truly lived. Social media was causing depression, she always said, suicide. Thousands of girls. Yet I was in Jake's mouth, alive.

"You're perfect," he said and held up his phone. I sprawled on a burgundy booth for the photo, crossed my legs, angled my body to look curvier.

"Yeah, like that," Jake said. "Okay, now look up at the wall." I looked at cobwebs and cigarette stains, framed photographs of shirtless men in big hair, bell-bottoms.

Jake said, "Perfect." I put a finger in my mouth.

"Baby," he said, and I felt certain that this was who I could be, perfect, baby. Backed by one hundred thousand hearts.

JAKE LOWERED HIS phone, passed it to me, showed me myself on his screen. I looked better from his perspective; every raw image already filtered. I scrolled while he signed the credit card receipt, left an extra twenty-dollar bill. Then he took his phone back and went to the bathroom with it. I stayed at the booth with mine, taking selfies next to photographs of Slash, Alice Cooper, Axl Rose. My kiss-kiss faces beside their guitars, voices, songs. I turned my phone to see myself. Here where my eyes were half shut, here where they were wide, here where I had tipped my chin and found the angle I knew was mine. I felt Jake arrive then, felt his hand on my shoulder and put my phone away, stood up, faced him. He turned me back around, gave my body a soft push in the direction of the door. He kept hold of my arm and steered me.

"I got it," I said, and pulled away. I wasn't a pushover. I was special, self-assured; it was important Jake know that. But resisting him was the wrong thing to do. His body stiffened. So in the car, I left my phone in my clutch, put a hand on his inner thigh, and looked him in the eyes and this made up for it. Because he opened his gated complex in Beverly Hills, his apartment, his bedroom for me like he couldn't believe his luck.

"I just bought this place," he said. "It's like, a work in progress." I crossed the threshold ahead of him, thinking as I did about childhood lessons: never get into a stranger's car, never go into their house, never give it up for a guy you don't love. But I wasn't a child. I wasn't a virgin. I already knew things. Womanly things, like love is overrated and pleasure is a right.

In Jake's room there were red dimmer lights, a mirrored wall. He sat on the bed and I fingered the straps of my silver dress, watching myself in the mirror. The beauty I saw was both familiar and new, like a twin I'd only just encountered, the one girl Jake had chosen from the endless scroll, those endless crystal faces. I slipped one strap, then the other off my shoulders and turned to him. In red, he looked lit up from the inside. He reached for me like I was glowing too and I glanced again at the mirror, myself, saw my own power fracture in the light, the room, the wall of reflective glass.

WHEN LEAH AND I were kindergarteners her parents (oil people, always working) paid my mother (single, a part-time librarian and sometimes dog sitter) to nanny their only child. And so it was the three of us before bed each night, my mother reading stories, turning pages and unlocking smells: Ivory soap, rosemary shampoo, Calvin Klein Euphoria. She chose only grown-up books, books she felt she needed—*The Bloody Chamber*, *Feminist Fairy Tales*, *Women Who Run with the Wolves*. We girls were too young for them, probably. They scared us, taught us. Through them we learned that although women are culturally conditioned to be nice, we are actually fierce. Prince Charming is an archetype, not a literal prince;

he is alive within us, and so is true love's kiss, sacred intuition, instinct. Our task is to reclaim our power, not bury it in the service of some man. My mother explained this to us before bed, sheets made into mountains by our knees, books open before us. But after, when the books were closed and the light was shut, we heard the crunch of gravel, the front door open for this boyfriend, or that one, men she met in doctors' offices and NA meetings, recovering addicts all. On nights like that we girls knew to stay quiet, stay sleeping, no shenanigans allowed. We understood it wasn't easy for my mother to live without wanting. Sex, protection, something to cut the pain. The pain was everywhere, my mother said, leftover from the cancer she survived when I was one. A full remission, a miracle. Still, scars remained, shaped like an ache only pills could dull. And so opioids, addiction, another illness, also deep, rooted in grief and shame and endless empty regret. She went to rehab when I was two, and again the year after. Second time, she did the work, discharged with resolve. And still my father left us, left her trying to soothe herself with everything other than the drugs she was forbidden. She tried CBD and feverfew. Acupuncture. A filter on the tap to take the fluoride out. She tried NA and EMDR. And she tried men. The dates she went on were often bad. When Leah and I were eleven, she quit them entirely. But this did not take the ache away, nothing did. Not even the internet, all that information, those answers she searched it for. What to do about loneliness? What to do about addiction? The perils of pesticides, phones. She joined Facebook groups for concerned parents, bookmarked articles about body image, campus sexual assault, our changing attention spans, brain tumors from cellular waves. Some of it turned out to be fake news, some of it didn't. None of it mattered to me. I had already decided to be different. If a powerful man chose me, it would give me power, too.

With Jake I was close to power, but not fully in possession of it, neither a child nor a woman, and not yet a wolf. It shocked me, to see myself entwined with a man, the lines of his body colored in and shaded. I watched us move together in the mirror, and thought of Marcus, my high school fuck buddy, his concave torso, skin stretched rice paper thin over the bones. With him, I had mostly felt uncomfortable, awkward and small. I had imagined him comparing me to the adult film actresses we both watched alone on our separate screens, their bodies efforted, like holes distressed into fake designer jeans. It was always about the women, then. Whether or not I was better than them. Sexier, but not sluttier, my wants smaller, my body smaller, though not too small.

But as Jake pulsed behind me, then from the side, then above, I began to feel sure that I was better than those women, sure that I was a body, a soul, that any man would gaze upon and see his own soul, reflected back. Jake watched his cock in the mirror, moving in and out, like he was watching a laptop screen, cocks moving in and out. I watched too. We were together in the glass, both of us enacting sensation, experiencing sensation. It was all the same, the performance, the reality.

"Baby," Jake said, "I'm coming."

"I want it," I said. It was the right thing to say. And it was true.

Jake's face snapped and he collapsed, lay still for a moment. Then he peeled away the condom, tossed it to the floor, turned so he could see us both in the mirror.

"You're so fucking gorgeous," he said and put his fingers in my hair. He went quiet after that, watching himself touch the beautiful girl. My heart pounded. But I hadn't come, hadn't expected to. This, Jake's pleasure, was better than orgasm anyway. Like a crime I'd gotten away with. And proof of what else I could pull off.

I WOKE IN Jake's bed the next morning, worried I'd left blood on the sheets. I had recently started a birth control pill designed to cut down on periods and never knew what to expect. I rolled to one side, checked for red, found only white, pulled tight. Except an empty space beside me, rumpled where Jake had slept. In the bathroom, the shower ran. I tiptoed to my tossed-off clutch, removed my phone, brought it back to bed. I checked my Instagram, found two hundred more likes. I checked the selfies I'd shot the night before, rolled over, checked the sheets again.

Before I started the pill, my periods had been irregular anyway. My mom took me to a stern gynecologist who said birth control was the only way to protect me from myself, the disordered eating habits she accused me of "courting."

"You could kill yourself," the doctor said, and I felt my brain go static. The rest reached me like a far-off channel, voices through the snow. *Early osteoporosis, infertility, heart problems.* "By thirty, you could be a hunchback," she said.

Jake's shower stopped. I put my phone on the bedside table, pulled the sheet off my naked body and arranged it to drape around me the way women in paintings and movies and magazine spreads were always draped, their breasts and bushes barely covered. My bush was stripped bare, anyway, barely recovered from the raw aftermath of my first wax, first act of self-care, self-directed violence. I shut my eyes, pretended to sleep.

With Marcus, I'd left a first-time gash on his bedspread, his parents out of town for the night. The next day he told me he'd had to douse the stain in bleach before his mother came home. I told him, whatever. "I'm so sorry for the inconvenience," I said, sarcastic. My mom had taught me not to be ashamed.

"The trick is to work up a good foam," she said the first time I awoke to rusty goop. For some reason, with her, it embarrassed me. Her soapy fingers in my blood.

"Oh honey," she said, "your body's just doing its job." Her face was calm, certain as she scrubbed. She seemed comforted by my body at work, recovering from colds and hay fevers; my body growth-spurting, bleeding, healing. I was different from her, I was healthy. We both wanted to believe that. But I couldn't seem to separate love from sameness. I was different, so I had to leave.

Jake said, "Hey baby." I opened my eyes. He said, "I want to be out in the world with you," and took me to a coffee shop full of girls. Girls on their phones while they waited on their orders, girls whose hungover beauty was careless and slouched, girls with their arms and legs flung wide, their mouths yawning. I tightened against them.

"What kind of milk you like, babe?" Jake said.

"Almond, please."

He kissed my nose, mimicked my voice—*almond, please*—and ordered for us both. When we left he held the door for me. For all the girls to see.

HE DROPPED ME at my Airbnb. The foyer, full of shoes. The common area, strewn with laundry. Someone had left a big sketchpad and caboodle of art supplies on the couch. I borrowed the pad, a few paintbrushes, and took them to my room, leaned a blank page against the wall, set up my selfie ring and went lampshade to lampshade, fiddling to get the light right. I sat on the floor with my props and picked up my phone, opened Instagram. I typed Leah's handle in the search bar. She had 365 followers and a feed full of landscapes, animals and food. Unreal expanses of earth she tagged #Aussie. #Kangaroos, #Koalas, #Beaches. There was a burger without the bun, a perfect, unbitten burrito, the Sydney Opera House. It seemed intentional, the absence of her body, and had since the day she left. Freshman year of high school, her parents relocated from Houston to Australia, another oil hub. A sudden promotion, an unexpected move. Every day since then, I'd looked for her on Instagram. As if any image I found could return me to the real girl, anyway. Leah, who chewed with her mouth open and got food stuck in her braces. Leah who twerked poorly when she danced and laughed from her torso, gruff, like a man. Leah who was a know-it-all. Leah who was sometimes secretive. And yet her body was my body's imperfect twin. The sweat and stick of it, the sweat and stick of mine. Nights of our girlhood we slept back-to-back in my bed, no space between us, no screens. Only the bunch of long nightgowns around our middles, the soft shell of Leah's butt, pressed against mine. It was sometimes difficult to tell where she ended and I began.

My mother was the one to remind us. To parse the differences in our personalities: Leah's, obsessive and extreme, focused on animals, sports, the great beyond. And mine: scared sometimes, sometimes needy, but happy with the safety of my world, the best friend I shared it with, the mother who pointed out our diverging bodies like she was trying to warn us we would someday grow apart. Which, of course, we did.

I put the phone down, took off my top. I forked paintbrushes between the fingers of my left hand, picked up my phone again with my right and snapped a selfie of my artist self. In Facetune, I softened my skin to a poreless sheen; I snatched my waistline, my jawline. I applied a grainy filter, to simulate the skin texture I'd erased, then arranged the edited image in the square of a new post. "The Artist's Way," I wrote for a caption.

I knew how trolls would respond, knew better than to engage

with them the way I used to, the way I knew they wanted me
to when they said—

@Super_mom_mel213: clothes please 🐷
@Lorainne-TX4ever: why you feel the need to degrade
your body this way?
@nolachica333: Shame on you
@carmella_paul: your narcissism is out of control 💂 💂 💂

—I also knew my mother would agree with them. The week
before I left for LA, she sat across from me at the kitchen table,
poking her phone with a pointer finger as if examining the
aftermath of something violent. When she turned it toward
me, my own account was on the screen, like evidence.

"You look angry here," she said. "I know Instagram is a
'business venture,' but I'm concerned you're slipping into a
disconnected place." She removed her glasses, touched her
face. "I will not let that happen. I'm going to keep an eye on
this from now on."

She had started her own account. Her handle was @Nau-
rene48. Her profile was blank, just an anonymous, disembodied
head, belonging to a man. Only sometimes did she show up on
my feed, not often enough for me to worry about her presence
there. "I'm out doing other things," I imagined her saying.
"Real things," real life. Sorting library books and issuing cards.
Sipping cold decaf coffee from the special Starbucks mug I'd

given her for Christmas. Cleaning the car. Depositing pay-checks at the bank in person, still distrusting of the mobile app; "real things."

@Naurene48 did not comment on my Artist's Way post. It was a hit—

@tinsley_dohertay: You r my idol 🙄🙄💜
@Imaobsessed: Babe 😍🔥😍🔥
@shugcloudlyfe: Damn 💯
@kellydae405: You're a work of art 💯🖤
@crazyjkid5.0: Gawd!
@Taylorleanne: This is a VIBE 🔥🔥🔥🔥
@thisisnikkiZ: So hot! 🔥

Jake posted an hour later like an answer. "Gorgeous night," he wrote beneath a tagged photo of me at the Rainbow Room. My silver dress caught the low light, glimmer filtered. 27,468 likes. I watched them tick. 32,000, 36,700, 40,100. They grew with a sick speed, real and thrilling and never enough.

IN THE MORNING I took a Lyft back to Jake's condo and signed his contract. My name, my initials, dashed care-lessly across the screen of an iPad, made him my manager. To celebrate, we shot content at his rooftop pool, first just me in a black bikini, then in a red bikini, then with a girl named Ella who provided the bikinis. Ella was Jake's client, too. She had 320,000 followers and was in her late twenties but didn't look it. She looked like money, lean and round in only the right places, with a gap between her two front teeth she said she'd had filed by a cosmetic dentist in Beverly Hills. "Guys lose their shit over it," she said, which, when I followed her on Instagram and scrolled her likes and comments, seemed to be true. But both on the gram and IRL Ella had a boyfriend, an Instagram-famous photographer, known mostly by his handle, @Chrisss. He and Jake instructed poses suggestive of girl-on-girl action, everything twinned but slightly othered: Ella's full body against mine, pitted; Ella's ease with the men and their camera, my discomfort with Ella, the tangerine one-piece she wore, somehow sexier than all my skin.

"Pretend it's just us," she said, but that made me worse.

"Anna, loosen up," @Chrisss said. "You look like you don't want it."

Jake came at me with a vape. "Babe, you need some weed," he said. I inhaled, exhaled, and felt extra aware of my body beside the other girl's. When what I needed was to forget us both.

Ella said, "Try like I'm one of them, like I'm a man." It was a game I had played with Leah when we were small, the two of us taking turns becoming the desirous guy—*Rhett*, was our name for him—who had a knack for throwing nameless female characters against walls and kissing them there, the violence thrilling and oddly familiar.

"You're a man," I said and sat on the pool's edge. I dipped in my legs and watched them distort with sun and water. Ella crouched behind me, touched my cheek. I turned, made my eyes a question. The camera fluttered. Ella leaned to my ear. It fluttered again. "You're so hot," she whispered and I would have told her no, you are, if she were still herself. But she was a man, so I touched her like I knew she wanted me. She slid into the pool, slid me in too.

"Kiss," I said and we did.

"Money shot," @Chrisss said, and showed the camera screen to Jake. The pictures were perfect, Jake said, "Très *Wild Things*," just what we needed.

WE ATE THAT night at El Coyote, site of Sharon Tate's last meal. I ordered a salad, swallowed my last birth control pill with a vodka soda. Ella was herself again. She ate guacamole with a fork.

"I'm off gluten, corn and cheese," she said. "I used to be able to eat whatever, but now I'm on an elimination diet."

"What's that?" I asked.

"There's something wrong with me, like inside." She waved her fork. "I have all these crazy symptoms, and the doctor says it's nothing, and I know it's not, so I'm thinking it's maybe dietary, I don't know, we'll see."

"Sorry," I said. My phone was facedown on the table and I flipped it over, checked the time, my notifications, looking for @Naurene48, both relieved and irritated when she wasn't there. If I had to hear about anyone's mysterious ailments, I'd rather it be my mom's. Endless and familiar, they'd given structure to my life. Not that my life in Los Angeles was unstructured. It was adventurous, on the way to lucrative. Which was what I'd wanted, wasn't it?

Jake paid the bill and I went home with him. He opened his laptop, double clicked a video of two girls orbiting a man like ecstatic satellites. We fucked to the sound of their pleasure, my voice in competition. After, we lay on our backs on the bed, Jake's arm a nook and me inside.

"Would you help me with something?" I asked.

He said, "Of course, baby."

"Now that I'm not at my job, I don't have health insurance, and I'm just out of birth control, and I know condoms suck." Truth was, I had always been jobless and my mom had dropped me from her shitty Library policy, trying to set an ultimatum and make me stay home, go to college, veer from the path I'd chosen.

"I was wondering what you think I should do."

He kissed my head. "I'll take care of it," he said. In the morning he made a call and set up an appointment for me to get an IUD and STD check. "Wait, what exactly is an IUD again?" I asked and he said, "Don't worry, it's easy, you'll see." He texted Ella to drive me. We sat in the waiting room of a pink clinic in Westwood and scrolled our phones until a nurse said my name and I stood.

"Good luck," Ella said. "It'll make everything easier."

"You're not coming?"

"I'm good," she said, eyes still on her screen. "I don't need to see that."

"See what?" I started, but the nurse was already leading me away.

It was only my second time in the stirrups. I didn't know what to expect and took a selfie on my back to distract myself. I was editing it for my story when the doctor came in and caught me. "You'll have to put that away, hon," she said. I hit post and tucked my phone under my butt.

"Scoot forward," she said. I moved and the phone moved with me. She reached inside. "Nice and small." She held up a copper T, tall as a razor blade. "Paragard insertion is a pinch, over in a pinch," she said. "Here's my hand, here's the device."

Pain grasped my low back, fist tight. Beneath me, my phone vibrated notifications, story replies, 😂, 😮, 😳, 😰, 👏, 🔥, 🎉, 💯. I counted every buzz. I focused on the hum of all that love and tried not to cry about the rest.

"All done," the doctor said, but the hurt still squeezed.

After, for a treat and a distraction, Ella and I took Jake's credit card to a hair salon where she had her curls relaxed and I dyed my mushroom-brown hair a rich espresso, Jake's idea. "Get a color all your own," he'd suggested, neither Kardashian black, nor platinum Playboy blond. Ella and I sat side by side, eyes on our phones, hair wrapped in foil, and she talked about her game plan, how she wanted to become a manager like Jake, travel the world, maybe start a podcast production company to promote her clients. "You need a next thing," she said, "for when you get older like me." I shrugged, tried to imagine aging. I tried to imagine 100,000 followers, 320,000 followers, the products I'd sell them, the trips I'd take, all expenses paid. But I couldn't picture what travel abroad looked like beyond vague images ripped from magazines in doctors' offices. Azure water, white and pink stucco, wreaths of marigolds. I wanted to see it for myself. "You ever get paid to go places?" I asked. Ella snorted. "All the time. The most amazing parties." I tried to imagine those, too.

AFTER THE SALON, we posed our blowouts in front of a pink wall on Melrose Avenue. Ella said it was famous. "Everyone gets a selfie here," she said. "It's like, an initiation." I leaned against the wall, flipped my hair. "Snatched," she said, and "MOM," and "gorg." I took her place behind the camera, eager to say the same for her, eager to be initiated. As we worked, I could feel myself bleeding from the procedure. That was normal, the doctor had said. But I looked pale in the pictures, wrung out against the bright backdrop. Jake said so too. "My little vampire," he said when I got back to his place and showed him. He said the pink wall was played out anyway and didn't mention my hair. I deleted the images, lowered my phone.

"I feel like garbage," I said and touched my free hand to my belly, where the pain was. "But Ella was so supportive, and she's so pretty." I lifted my phone again, looked at its face, pretending there was something there. I meant for Jake to compare us and say I was the hot one.

"Right?" he said. "Open up." He placed a white circle on my tongue.

"What's this?" I said, jaw hanging, chemical slow-melting.

"Percocet for the pain," he said. I thought of my mother and swallowed anyway.

"Go rest," Jake said. I put myself on the couch, tucked up my feet, and checked my comments—

@vayscorpio: you're the best and I can't stand iiiittttttttttttt

@Naurene48: Can u show your unfiltered face please?

@brittanychill: that waist 💯

@sskintagram: nice. 😍😍😍

@sskintagram: 🔥💯😍😍🖤🖤🖤

@sskintagram: hi there! DM to collab 🌿

@giancarlobat4: ciao sei fantastica complimenti 🌿🌷🖤

@yogirealone: if you zoom in u can see the Photoshop

@reuben_dregsa: hot 🔥🔥🔥🔥

@day078: beautiful! 🔥

I checked my DMs. *Hey, what's up, sexy, let's collab*, offers Jake said I'd never need now that I had him. He brought me a bowl of chicken soup. He brought me tea, a hot water bottle I held skin to skin, like a newborn. The broth and bottle, the pill, forced loose the fist inside me and I dissolved into the couch, into Jake, cross-legged at my side, laptop in his lap. "Check it out," he said, and showed me the site where he bought legit fake followers. "They'll like your posts and never fall off." He pressed the button and delivered me to their love.

"I'm a star," I slurred, and I was right. By the morning, the number 50,000 had appeared beneath my name, both prosthetic and true.

5.

So, we needed content to feed my new followers. Where better than Vegas? Jake said. Shots of the casino, dinner at Momofuku, glamorous images to earn follows, sponsors, hearts. He drove, I sang *Vegas Baby* to the camera, and posted. Two hundred likes, 427, 600. The sun set and we chased it. Ninety-seven miles per hour, 100, 103. Dark desert and then, from nothing, a glittering motherboard. We descended into that bright home.

On the strip, I looked out the window, elevated, separate from the wheels of light and color, the vans advertising backpagepro.com, Spearmint Rhino, Chippendales, Criss Angel, Cirque du Soleil; the gamblers in tracksuits and sweats, backpacks and visors; a team of high school athletes in slide sandals and pajama pants. All those bodies in close proximity, overwhelming in their press. My first summer with Leah, when we were both five years old, my mom took us to Galveston during high season. The Pleasure Pier was pumped with music and tourists, whose nearness made me small. Engulfed, I couldn't breathe. It was a feeling I recognized from the nightmares I was prone to, dreams of thoughtless crowds enveloping and erasing me. I sat down on the sidewalk with my head between my knees, Leah trying to calm me with knock-knock jokes I didn't answer, my mother a shield, a wreath of smells: hand sanitizer, Euphoria, secret deodorant and beneath it, sweat.

"Count, Anna," my mom instructed. I felt her fingers on my forehead, brushing away the hair, then wrapped around the clench of my hand. *One, two, three*, she sang, a technique learned from her latest self-help quest: a book, a course, an anonymous meeting of addictive personalities. Leah recited the numbers too. I followed with my breath. The panic became sub-perceptual. Afterward, I felt older and hungry. My mom bought beignets and rifled around in her giant purse for wet wipes when the powdered sugar stuck to our lips. We got in the car and drove, looking for a plot of quiet beach. On the edge of town, we found it, a spot we returned to every summer, Leah and I swimming, snacking, bearing our backs for my mother's excessive sunscreen application. We were twelve when Instagram started, fourteen when we got phones and I made @annawrey. The first image I shared was the last one my mother took of Leah and me, the last summer at our spot, both of us bikini-clad and Paris-filtered, posed before the ocean's gray scroll. At the time, the post earned ten likes. But in LA, with Jake, everything was growing, and every day love for that first picture ticked upward, too. A hundred, three hundred, six hundred, a thousand.

AT THE MANDALAY Bay, we climbed from the Rover, into the teem. The valet took Jake's keys, accepted his tip. The travelers and gamblers and babies and janitors and sightseeing guides and toy poodles pushed in. I unlocked my phone.

My mother had called during the drive, and texted: "Who is that girl you are with on your account?" She wrote: "Where were those photographs taken and by whom?" I felt dread wash up inside me. I had meant to block @Naurene48 from seeing my recent stories, the shots of Ella and me by the pool, *très Wild Things.*

"I'm fine!" I texted back. "Don't be dramatic, luv u, call u soon."

I pressed send and trotted to keep up with Jake, striding forward through the throngs, the casino where tourists milled or sat at the slot machines, pulling levers, pressing buttons. Hundreds of eyes turned to see us. The carpet slowed the wheels of my suitcase and my shoulders caught the drag, rolled in, protective as the folded wings of a sleeping bat.

We walked down the hallway that separated the Mandalay—built fourteen years before and already shabby—from the Delano, its newer, boutique counterpart. A relief, to exit the lights of the casino, the eyes, the oxygenated air. A relief, to stand by the window of our white suite on the twenty-sixth floor and look down on the strip, the bodies of its patrons erased by distance. I counted breaths, focused on that distance—my body from the crowd, my body from the ground, from Leah, our spot on the beach, my mother in a ridiculously large sunhat, spreading out a blanket. I took a picture of my reflection, distant lights inside me and beyond. And Jake, stepping into the background, wrapping his arms around my waist, both of us high and safe, conjoined. He unzipped my jeans. His fingers moved inside me and the heel of his hand pressed a dull ache into my whole body, a thick stamp, marking me his.

Downstairs, he shot Vegas content of me in my silver dress, leaning over the craps table, sitting at the slots, hand on the lever. He instructed every pose, even outtakes, blurry images of my teeth and smile; a picture with a bite of ribeye lifted to my mouth. We left too much steak on our plates when we finished. We ran through the casino holding hands and it was like running through sand, a crowded beach, bodies to weave in and out of, eyes that turned to watch us. It was possible that Jake was in love with me. Was I in love with him? Possibly. If he was. I imagined a chapel, an Elvis impersonator, candy rings and sincere words. But I couldn't marry Jake, couldn't marry anyone. Marriage was a cage, a career killer for someone young like me; if Jake asked, I would have to say no. I would have to call my mother. I would have to return. Home to where coupons were clipped and portions were weighed, for the sake of waistlines and wallets. It felt for a moment like relief, to have to go back, to have no other choice.

But the car Jake ordered took us to a club, not a chapel. Cavernous and dark and full of naked women. They danced on a stage shaped like a spilled drink, all those round and seeping circles. Jake said, "No phones here, babe," and I put mine in its clutch.

He bought a table, led me to it, and we sat in a pair of plush chairs. The women danced, appearing and disappearing through fake fog and lights, like specters in a dark wood. I stood. I would join them. Jake told me to sit.

"Only the girls can dance," he said. "But here." He pulled a vial from his pocket, twisted the cap. A lever unfolded from the top and became the smallest spoon. He dipped the spoon, removed a mound of powder from the vial, showed me how to bump it. It was my first time doing cocaine.

"Tip your head back," he said and lifted my chin with his fingers like I was a kid with a nosebleed. I tasted chemical drip. My throat felt full and numb. Every month or so my mom would drink too much Yellow Tail and talk about my dad's coke habit, the powder he hid in his sock drawer, how he'd cut lines before business meetings and dinner parties. I could see her, balled up on the sofa, sipping her Chardonnay—the one controlled substance she didn't avoid—her crew-socked feet tucked under her butt. "He was always looking for escape," she'd say on nights like these, evidence that losing him wasn't her fault only.

Jake's eyes drifted to the stage.

"I have to pee," I said and walked to the women's restroom, found it empty. I checked my phone. There wasn't service and I put it away, widened my mouth for the mirror. My throat was open. I was fine. I swallowed, touched my face, my neck, and it was like touching another girl's face or neck, smooth and unfamiliar, and this time, I was the confident one. I swung through the door and into the hallway. I found an ATM and fed it my debit card. Jake had been paying for everything, and I wanted him to pay. Moving to LA had cost me; my phone bill, my six-week stay in the Airbnb, paid upfront and in full, had cost me. I selected "check balance." I only had four hundred and seventy-six dollars left. Unless Jake got me a sponsorship and I earned enough, and quickly, I wouldn't have a place to stay. As it was, since he messaged me, I had slept most nights at his condo.

I pictured my mom again, seated at the computer in the kitchen this time, checking her accounts. The room came into focus in fragments: her coffee cup, filmy with cream; her stacks of unpaid bills, coupons, bank statements. She had four credit cards, each one always spent to the limit. The child support money, like her paycheck, was never enough and when I turned eighteen, it had run out anyway. She dog sat sometimes after that but cut her customers too many deals and we argued about it.

"You don't value your time," I often said. Her response was always the same: "Honey, I am many things, but a user isn't one of them."

The machine asked if I needed more time. I pressed no and returned to the table. Jake was with a woman. The sight of her, swaying in front of him where I belonged, made me swallow hard over a choke. I sat and she swayed in my direction, too. Jake said, "You can touch her," and then, "I want to see you touch her." The woman came close and I touched her with only my fingertips.

"You're fine, baby," she said and straddled my chair. I put my hands on her waist.

Jake passed me the vial and I snorted. He passed me a wad of dollar bills and I fed them to the dancer's G-string with care, and then, with less of it. She put her nose in my neck like she was kissing me there. A simulated gesture, but it did something for Jake. He leaned to my other ear, fit it in his teeth. The song wound down.

"Thirty for another," the dancer said.

"We're good, baby," I said and she dismounted. Jake tipped her, a new song began, mean and big-beated. He said, "Fuck that was hot," and took more coke, dipped the spoon again for me. "Now I want to see you with other guys," he said as I bumped. "I want to see you fuck the whole world."

IN THE MORNING Jake called for a late checkout. I woke to the sound of him, thanking the front desk clerk, hanging up the phone.

"Morning, baby," he said to me and stood, started moving around, packing up.

"Hey," I managed through the anger darting around inside me, a fighting fish in its miniscule bowl. I felt dramatic about it and searched my mind for its source. After the club, Jake had fucked me sweetly, like he knew he should reassure me I was enough for the time being, no others needed. But that was it, the anger was on behalf of the others, the *babies*, the women from the club. Pointless, I thought, to feel anything on their behalf, condescending. The strippers were just doing their jobs; sex work was a choice and should be decriminalized, normalized. This was the feminism that empowered me, too.

On the drive back to Los Angeles, we passed Jake's vape back and forth.

"Just stoned," I said when he asked what I was thinking. But I was still thinking about the club, what Jake had said in the drunk dark—*now I want to see you with other guys*. Sex positivity meant I shouldn't judge his polyamory either. But I had planned to use him, and to use him I needed him to want only me, only for himself, an object of his own to show the world, but never let them have. Somewhere in this game, I had already fucked up.

"You'll stay over, right?" he said as we got close to the city. He put a hand on my hand and I made a fist. He picked up the fist and licked it. In the garage, he drew a cover over the car. In the elevator, we kissed.

"Stay all weekend," he said into my mouth. "Water my plants." In the morning, he was flying to Arizona for a night. "Stay forever," he whispered and I felt my body give, every muscle relaxing, like a pill had kicked in. He opened the front door, dangled the key at me. I looked at myself in the hallway mirror, then followed him to the living room.

"Stop," he said, and I did. He crossed the room, sat on the couch. "Get on all fours."

I just stood there. "Why?" I asked and he smirked but didn't answer. Slowly, I lowered to my knees. "Beg me," I said, and he said, "No," and the smirk became a grin.

I waited for him to speak again. When he didn't, I crawled toward him.

"Good girl," he said.

WE WENT TO bed early. Sometime in the night, I thought I felt Jake kiss my forehead. But I woke alone.

I made a nest of sheets and pillows and hid inside it with my phone. Jake had airdropped me the Vegas images; we'd set a post-time, and a caption, *Luck Be a Lady*. In my favorite picture, I leaned over the craps table. The silver dress drooped at the bust, my clavicle jutted forward. The bones looked beautiful, expensive, like pieces of an antique ship, graceful and worth naming. I edited my jawline to a heart shape, filtered my skin to a textureless glow. I closed the picture, opened it again, to see it as a follower would, then replaced some of the texture, and posted. I left my nest, walked around the condo, opening drawers and doors. I sat on Jake's toilet watching Instagram. The stories feature was less than a year old, but already it had changed the way I shit. I ate one of Jake's low-carb collagen breakfast bars, which tasted like glue. I made coffee with his Nespresso and imagined breaking it. When I checked my phone again, I had seven hundred likes, one hundred comments, and a voicemail from my mom:

"Anna, I need to get on the phone with you. I've been

looking at your Instagram as it seems to be the only way for me to know what's going on. You look sick in your latest post, and unhappy. Are you making money yet? Where are your girl-friends? Where are you? When I call, you don't pick up. When I text, you take days to answer. I feel very out of control when it comes to your health and I need to make contact. Call me as soon as you get this."

I thought, or you'll do what? Then I imagined my mom at Jake's front door, pounding. It would be almost funny to see her there, frizzy-headed, dog hair on the butt of her *Not Your Daughters* brand jeans. Maybe I missed her. Maybe I wanted her to come. I didn't know what I wanted. I had thought I knew. I opened Lyft but didn't know where to go, where I could afford to go. I had recently watched a story Ella posted in which she and her mom shopped at a mall called the Beverly Center. It would cost me thirteen dollars to get there. I scheduled the ride, gathered my stuff, and left.

THE MALL WAS like the Houston Galleria, where my mom would take Leah and me back-to-school shopping. A familiar space, the couture clustered at the top; the middle floor, bookended by department stores, Abercrombie and Zara and Victoria's Secret in between; the basement where the bargains lived. My mother didn't understand "fancy designers." We shopped at JCPenney on the lowest, darkest level. But at the Beverly Center, I wandered in and out of Gucci, Prada, Saint Laurent like I knew their worth, and mine. Men stared.

They held the hands of women who also stared, especially the older ones. They made me think of the crescendo of my mother's menopause, ongoing as I prepared to leave for LA, as we argued over my leaving, as finally, she let me go, lingering in the doorframe of my room, frozen peas pressed to her chest, watching me pack.

"It'll be a relief, the end of all that," she said, cryptically.

"All what?" I said, annoyed to have to ask for context, annoyed to indulge her.

"Being looked at," she said. "Not that I'm looked at much as it is, but from now on it'll be just me, no men to show off for."

"I'm not showing off for men," I said.

"That's not what I'm saying," she said. And then, innocently, she asked, "But isn't that what Instagram is all about?"

"Um, no," I said.

"What are you doing when you post, then?"

"Wow," I said. "Misogynist much?"

And yet it did feel like an accomplishment, to take the attention of other, older women's men. Also, lonely. I wandered around the Beverly Center, watching my reflection in every window, a small, solitary girl projected over shoes, bags, lush swathes of leather and silk. Meaningless objects next to the young, white beauty I wore as a pass, permission to enter and browse. Still, I was aware of the scratched pleather backpack I used as a purse, the silver clutch I carried at night, their cheap sameness in every picture I shared.

I felt better at Bloomingdale's. I boarded the escalator, put

my phone in selfie mode, star filtered, and filmed myself riding
downward, past the Juniors' floor, the Women's. I pursed my
lips, turned my head one way, then the other, like I was showing off diamond baguettes, not tarnished Target hoops. On
the Contemporary floor, I got off and walked in circles. In
my normal life I wore jeans, jean shorts in the summer, white
T-shirts. Now I wanted something else, a black silk clutch, not
designer, but nice enough to look like it. And a black bodycon
dress I thought Jake would like. I took them to an empty fitting room.

The dress was tight in the ass, loose in the bust. I spun for
the mirror's flattering light, shot a selfie in the trifold glass. In
it I looked bored and thirsty. I turned again, posed again. The
mirror was like a door in the wall. Beyond it, a void that sucked
me back to the beige JCPenney fitting room where my mom
vetoed the crop tops me and Leah were suddenly into.

"These are for older girls, girls," she said, the tags flipped
over in her fingers. It was what she would say of this dress, too.
I sent Jake the best selfie I could take. "What up playa 🎤?" I
wrote and waited for his response.

The summer of the crop tops was the summer Leah opened,
sudden as a night-blooming flower, into a pair of D-cups
nobody knew what to do with. I didn't envy her. I wanted to
be modelesque, thin and willowy, pliable. It seemed safer than
what Leah had. The year before that, when we both turned
ten and she got her period, it had frightened us both. Leah
had been particularly avoidant: thick white pads with gashes

of blood in the middle littered the bedroom like slain bodies, curled in on themselves and left on the battlefield to rot. The mess was aggressive, as if Leah was angry at someone, something, for butting in on her childhood. But when her breasts came, when men began to honk their horns as we walked the neighborhood, or once, stopped us at Starbucks and offered to buy our Frappuccinos, she indulged them like it was her job. Like *indulger of men* was a character for her to play, a woman, tinged with rage.

MY PHONE BUZZED. Jake wrote, "Hey giiiiiirl, you should get that, how much? I'll send." I craned my arm to find the tag. It tongued my skin, rough when I removed it. The original price was hidden by a sale sticker that said $499.00. *Fuck*, I whispered, and peeled the sticker off, found $900.00. I was sweating when I took a picture of the high number and sent it to Jake.

"You surrrreeee?" I wrote. Four hundred extra would get me shoes, too, and the black bag.

Another buzz with a notification: *Jake Alton has sent you $900.00.*

"Worth it, don't bug about the comments on ur post," he wrote.

I sent him 😭😭😭 and went straight to the comments—

@Naurene48: Call your mother, Anna.
@anylonelyshark: lol 🙃

@soccermami: yeaaaa, what would your mother say?

@ronnguyy: leave her alone haters, she's gorgeous

@Naurene48: Anna, you need to call me.

@jessajack27: omg 😂😂😂

@witchcraft1998: she looks stoned

@beccatorres: girl, call your mom

@deesousa: call her

@Naurene48: Call your mother or these comments persist.

I held my phone at arm's length. I was going to cry and didn't want to. Nor did I want to block my mother. Nor did I want to call her and listen to her anger, her fear, her threats. But I needed to make her comments stop. I rushed out of the dress, out of the room, to the register. I stood in line, fidgeting, and watched Leah's story. "Morning run 😂😂🏃" it said with a picture of a trail that snaked along the ocean.

The shoppers ahead of me took their receipt and walked off, loaded with bags. I put the dress on the counter with the clutch and the saleswoman scanned the tags, then my phone. She watched the computer monitor. We waited. I was sweating, nervous. About the expense of the dress? About tricking Jake into buying it? About my mother?

"Is there another payment method we can use?" the saleswoman asked.

"I'd rather not," I said and she sighed, reached for the phone again, scanned it again. I counted breaths, imagined grabbing the dress and running. Somewhere far, so the saleswoman couldn't find me. Somewhere my mother couldn't find me, either.

"Okay, it went through. Can I get you a garment bag?"

"That's okay." I smiled to make up for my clipped tone.

"Are you sure, hon?"

I said yes and she began to wrap the dress. "I'm in a rush," I added, and the saleswoman quickly folded it into a bag she handed over, no eye contact.

I walked to a set of couches outside the Bloomingdale's entrance, touched my mom's number on my phone and counted the rings. They seemed timed to match my heartbeat.

"Anna." Her voice through the fuzz of Bluetooth and distance was sudden. I woke to it with a jerk and tried to speak, but nothing came out.

"Honey," she said.

"Mom," I managed.

"We have to talk," she said. "I'm late to an appointment, though. I'm walking in right now, I'll call you back in an hour." I heard the phone switch over from Bluetooth. A voice in the background said, "Checking in?" and my mom whispered, "Yes."

"Okay?" she said to me. "It's important, okay?"

I said okay and she said okay, then we hung up. When she called me back, I was picking out shoes. I didn't answer.

6.

Jake flew home from Arizona, sunburned, to attend a party he called an opportunity. "The house is sick," he said. "Wear your new dress, we'll get good content." Before we left, we stood in his bathroom, wrapped in towels, and I patted concealer over red patches on his face.

"How's that?" I asked. He turned to the glass, made a mirror face.

"You fixed me."

I dried my hair, took time with my makeup. I put on the black dress, the heels, put lip gloss and liner in my new black clutch, took a selfie, deleted it. The light at Bloomingdale's, the generous mirror, had masked the bodycon bust, deflated from the wrong angle. I went from Jake's bathroom mirror to his bedroom mirror, trying to see what the truth was. I smoothed the puckered fabric, twisted my torso, shot my reflection with the sexy bunny filter and shared it to my stories, which Jake said I needed more of. Stories were rawer than posts, more true. Stories showed life as it truly was, not like the grid where everything was painted over, robbed of any contrast, any ugly underbelly. I knew what he meant. My own grid looked so perfect as to be grotesque at times, my Photoshopped body leached of blood and shit and sweat, the thrill of knowing every beautiful body holds all that inside it.

Jake arrived behind me in the mirror. He'd put on a suit, slim cut and also black. He checked himself first, then me. He'd noticed neither the bag nor the heels I'd tricked him into buying, and the secret thrilled me.

"You look good," he said. I turned the word *good* around in my head. Good was not great, not stelle, stunning, beautiful, 🔥🔥🔥.

He said, "How do I look?"

"Good," I said.

Before we left, he cut us lines on a powder-smeared mirror, showed me how to use a straw like a hose, suctioning up the mess. I cleaned it and felt 🔥 for real. Then Jake pulled the cover off his Land Rover and we drove into the hills, to a house made of angles and roofs. Inside, people wore suits and dresses. A girl in a tuxedo tended the open bar. A fake fireplace licked fake flames. We stood in line for drinks and I checked my phone. Follows and hearts, flames in my DMs.

"No pictures," said the man ahead of us. He held a paper shopping bag.

"Sorry," I said and put the phone away.

"What's in the bag?" Jake asked. The man opened it up, showed us a colorful pile of dildos. Jake said "bro," and laughed.

I laughed too, but thought I sounded nervous. The man was with a woman, who gave me a long, wounded look.

"I forgot this was a sex party," Jake said when the couple walked off. His voice was nonchalant, and I made my face match it. "But we don't have to do anything, I just think the house is dope."

"It's dope," I said and went straight to the memory of Leah and me, belly down on my bed with her new laptop. Incognito mode, Pornhub, the main page peppered with America's most watched videos: *real teen anal, teen orgy, multi-squirt orgasm, extra small ten teen body.* "Gross," we said of these, even if in private, and with time, we would watch, inure ourselves, learn. But together, we made a game out of safer search terms. *Delivery guy, big boobs, blow job,* each one punctuated by Leah's throaty laugher.

Costumes was the word that found us "Masked Medieval Fuck Fest," a vintage orgy we watched under the guise of a joke and returned to so often we could recite its language. *Forsooth, thy cock is rock hard* and *what a bounteous bosom m'lady.* The film was good-humored raunch, a joke and a fantasy; but it had been viewed twelve thousand times, which meant it was also a possibility. Surely someone out there would make it real.

Jake led me outside. I posed in the backyard for him. There was a koi fish pool, stepping-stones across the water. I walked halfway out, teetering, and remembered reading somewhere that the males were biters, and dangerous. Jake said, "Tip your left hip, turn your head to the right." He said, "Do that again only don't smile." He said, "You look cold," and we went back inside. The house was empty.

"They're all upstairs," he said and ordered a shot, took it.

"I want to see," I said.

"You want to see, baby? You sure?"

I was sure. I wasn't a prude, wasn't a square. "Okay," Jake said, "bump up." He passed me the coke and we both did more. I put the vial in my clutch and he let me. When he wiped my nose, I felt his fingers tremble. "Let's just stick together," he said and I took his hand, which stilled in mine. We climbed the stairs.

Upstairs was wide open, a room not a hall, and nowhere a door. The room was strewn with mattresses, tissue boxes, bodies like forgotten toys, arms and legs tangled. I felt my hand go wet in Jake's. The bodies were moving. They were fucking, awkward in their conflicted rhythms. There was the man with the paper bag inside a girl I hadn't seen downstairs. There was his date, reverse cowgirl and the shape of a body beneath her in the shadows. The party was like "Medieval Fuck Fest," only no masks or minstrel music, no laughter, just moans and wet skin slapping; the party was just another club, stripped of another layer.

"Want to get out of here?" Jake whispered.

"We should join," I said, taking in the bodies, comparing them to my own, which was 🔥, I was certain of it. There was a chair in the center of the room, and I led Jake to it. He sat, I knelt. He looked down at me. The angle made him smaller. I opened my clutch, offered the coke.

"Let's stick to just each other," he said again as we bumped.

I said, "Of course, baby," and heard my voice, proud like I'd won something. He was soft and small in my hands. In my mouth, he hardened. Eyes turned to watch my work.

WHEN IT WAS over, when we turned to leave the room and all those bodies, I noticed a second space, an annex off the first, and stopped to peer in. More bodies, packed thick. Close where I could see, an older man fucked a woman who bent at the waist and mewled, hair over her face. A second woman embraced the man from behind. Still, he turned. From inside the heat and all that contact, he reached for me. His hand was wide and wanting. I felt myself smile the way people sometimes smile at tragic news, a sick, involuntary response, detached from how they really feel. My breath shortened, and I began to count. I left. But later, I wondered if I had wanted to stay. I wondered where my desire began, where Jake's ended.

I ask these questions often now that I'm alone.

PART TWO

7.

I wake in a frigid room. A muted TV beams unhappy light. I've been dreaming and inspect my body to remember what's real, where I am. Pleats in my skin from stiff sheets tell me: the princess-themed hotel in Burbank, the pool I lingered at all afternoon, the mother and daughter I followed; I am thirty-five, not nineteen, a woman, not a girl. I touch my phone. It's not yet late, though I have slept through dinner. I find the TV remote, press the volume, and voices rise up. *Your favorite childhood food items only elevated!* a host says. *Chicken and Stars*, a contestant answers, and background music brings the mood down. The TV flashes family photos as the contestant's disembodied voice talks about his sister's prolonged illness, her early death. *Our happiest memories took place in the kitchen*, he says.

I stare at the monotonous screen, walk behind my eyes through my mother's kitchen. The rice cooker and electric kettle, the microwave splattered inside with tomato sauce from the soggy English muffin pizzas she'd make for Leah and me after school. We'd sit at the blue-tile table, a hand-me-down from my grandmother. Our feet dangled from the chairs. Red sauce gathered in the corners of Leah's mouth and she never seemed to notice, or care. She cared about animals, habitats, the plight of the displaced sea turtle and horseshoe hare. And she cared about us, the world of us, filled with a language all our own, composed of voices, characters we'd made up: mean old "Farmer Cowhide's" country twang; high class "Queenie's" pitched whine; rakish "Rhett's" sleazy drawl. And "Doomer," a foreboding growl Leah assumed on the nights she tried to keep me awake.

"Wait, did you hear that?" Doomer would grunt, just as I was drifting to sleep. "There's someone in the house." A murderer, rapist, child molester.

"Don't get me riled up," I'd plead, truly afraid but also often giggling. We both knew she was faking. But sometimes we'd forget. Sometimes, as Doomer, Leah would scare us both so bad we'd call for my mom—*Mom! Naurene!*—who would arrive, annoyed to have to sit on the edge of the bed, keeping watch, until we fell asleep.

I get out of bed, shuffle to the bathroom, count my fifty Vicodin, sift pills like memories. The Galveston Pleasure Pier, beignets and sundresses. The summer Leah and I learned to dive, the summer of the sailor's bracelets that shrank around our wrists and were always damp. The summer we pooled our chore money to adopt an endangered red wolf named Granny, and all we received in return was a pamphlet showing Granny's picture, some facts about her life. Leah cried in frustration. She had imagined a forest ranger would deliver the old wolf in a crate, to live out the rest of her years in my mother's back-yard. "Granny's better off in the wild, honey," my mother said, wiping tear-sopped hair off Leah's face. "You wouldn't want to confine her to a pen." She made us English muffin pizzas, then put us to bed, and in the morning, Leah and I sat at the table and identified a new animal to advocate for and save (whales, it turned out).

I select the final pill, swallow, then sit on the princess pink toilet with my bathrobe bunched around me and tally phantom calories. A hundred and forty for the English muffin, seventy for the tomato sauce. Counting is an instinct I can't silence. Counting is like hunger itself. I used to think it would pro-tect me. As if in reducing the essence of something—a story, a meal, a body—to a number, I'd know its truest value.

I'm allotting two hundred calories for cheese when I hear knocking, pounding, heavy enough to shake the hotel fire door. I jerk upright and imagine men in sunglasses, men in masks, faceless men sent to silence me. I wipe fast, slide against the wall, put my eye to the keyhole. I see nothing and open the door a crack, then all the way. The vision was overblown. The hall is empty. The Vicodin has kicked in.

Sometimes when it goes to work, when it mixes with AMPs or benzos or whatever else, I see things, hear things, that aren't really there. A common side effect, like chemical drip or dry mouth. And worth it, to arrive in that permissive, powerful place I have always wanted to inhabit. Drugs erase time, age, mistakes; drugs don't work the way they used to. But they're better than nothing, the closest thing I've got now to what Instagram once promised.

I close the door, turn, un-turn, re-turn the bolt to make certain it's locked. I swing the safety latch, look again through the peephole, then return to the bathroom: my pill bottles and makeup and serums, the discarded bathing suit bottoms I didn't bother to pick up, the mirror I shouldn't face. I don't need to look to know I'm a mess. I bend down, scoop up the suit, hang it on the door handle, and turn to catch my reflection, pretty and pulled together. I lean toward the glass, make a kiss face and the reflection changes. I step back. "Don't start with this," I say aloud, though it's too late. Before my eyes, my face becomes a landslide, running downhill. There's filler under the skin, collected in the troughs. And still it falls. Doesn't it? I can't trust what I see, can never know what about me is real. Which laser facial designed to smooth fine lines and sun damage burned white ridges into my chin? I see them if I squint, don't I? Which dermal filler, and how much of it, migrated from my marionette lines and changed the mobility of my mouth? It slopes sadly now, incapable of smiling. And who botched my first nose job, who botched my second? Which strip-mall med spa, which injector, aesthetician, plastic surgeon—and there have been many—left a lip lift scar in the middle of my face?

My phone is by the toilet where I left it. I open the camera, take a selfie and pinch the screen to see myself, distorted, a Picasso muse, every flaw a drama. Is this how I really look? I often spend hours trying to know for certain. I press the shutter again, again, again, then step back and pinch the ugly selfies I just shot, parsing the distortion of the lens from past procedures, the passing of time.

"No way to *stop* time, but a good idea to try." This is what I tell my customers, women who come to see me in the black and white striped store where I wait for them.

I wait among the serums and sheet masks and red-light wands; the makeup named after Instagram filters I pat over eye bags and nasolabial folds.

"Not *anti*-aging, *graceful* aging," I say, and load women's shopping baskets with promises of transformation, erasure, control. Empty promises, I've always thought, illusory. The women shouldn't trust me. Even as a child, I believed the solution to age and plainness was to transform the body itself, not cover it; to shrink or expand as needed through starvation, exercise, the Adderall girls in my high school took to stay satiated and small, the injectables and surgery that came later. I never bought into the surface stuff: serums, creams, makeups. The only meaningful change comes from within, I still believe that.

But now, every answer, every solution, contradicts. I read recently that long-term benzo use, opioid abuse, leads to early dementia, perpetual forgetting. I read that Botox weakens the forehead; when it wears off, you look older than ever. I read that a frozen face has been proven to a make a woman happier than an expressive one; she looks in the mirror, sees less trouble, and becomes it. Before I left Texas, Houston, work, to come here, spring rains had started, torrential storms rising up out of nowhere, then gone again, the world washed and reeling in their wake. But the sky reverts to normal, like it has forgotten its rage. Like it never felt anything at all.

This is the best I can hope for, a clean slate before the next storm, next tragedy, next decade. My expectations are realistic. Realistic expectations are important for anyone contemplating cosmetic surgery. It's the people who want to look like someone else entirely—Kendall, Kylie, a Siamese cat—that get into trouble. I just want to look like myself, my true self, stripped of time and the violence of past mistakes.

So I'm here, in Los Angeles again, the only city in the world with Aesthetica™, performed only by Dr. Perrault, the only surgeon capable of undoing, in a single procedure, every procedure that came before. For now, anyway. I have read that infection rates are worse than reported, read the FDA is investigating Aesthetica™ and will pull it from the market any day. Because patients have suffered autoimmune responses, their body rising up to reject their new face; patients have suffered infection within the first twenty-four hours, the result of contaminated flesh, sepsis. There have been deformities. "Aesthetica™ erases everything," Dr. Perrault said during our virtual consult, "though as with any surgery there's risk involved." As if he had to say it. I booked the procedure then and there. I entwined myself, willingly, in a fast dance with death.

I DROP MY phone in the pocket of my robe, leave the mirror and move around the Princess Suite, tidying up. Plastic wrappings from coffee cups, the flip-flops I kicked off in different directions when I returned from the pool. I'll need the room neat and clean when I come back post-procedure. If I come back.

I'm gathering wet towels to pile by the door when light glints against the edge of my vision, refracted from the window's glass. I go to it. In the distant sky, a firework show has started. I watch for a moment. Explosions blossom like flowers on a nature show, fast forwarded from buds to full blooms. I rush to the bed, fish my phone from the messed-up sheets, take video I'll never watch. Certainly, I'll never post. Instagram is an app for bots and grandmas, now. It's been six years since I shared anything. Not that I don't want to. It's what I know @annawrey can't give me, after all this time.

The grand finale makes the sky a bouquet. It wilts into the dark. I open Instagram, fall belly down on the bed. I'm signed into a fake account and rather than log onto @annawrey, I search her as I would anyone I followed once, liked, then ghosted. She loads slow and outdated, a museum of my past selves, every image the remains of a girl, frozen in time, waiting for me to return and rescue her. There she is, high ponytail and puppy filter, riding shotgun in Jake's Land Rover. *Vegas baby*, she sing-songs. I watch her cut off and repeat, persistent as the lost, calling to be found.

AS A GIRL, I wanted to be discovered. Fifteen years later, as a thirty-five-year-old woman, I want to undo the past and disappear. And yet that reporter has found me. I could make a difference to other women, she writes, every time she DMs @annawrey asking for my story, my experience with Jake. She says a name like mine could help gather other names. "But the choice is only ever yours," she adds. As if she has to. Choice is a power I am well aware is mine to wield. A feminist, post-feminist right. To give my story, or keep it to myself, keep myself hidden and safe. My choice to surgically alter my body, impregnate my body, stay natural, stay alive, stop living.

For a moment, I try to consider the words I might use to come forward, where I'd begin, which transformations I'd include, which traumas, where I'd say they end. I try not to imagine Jake or his lawyers, what they would do to shut me up, the story they could make of me, so easy to discredit. But the opioids have pulled a shade down in my brain anyway. Around me, the Princess Suite has dissolved. I scroll the @annawrey museum. Hunger rises up, stoked by every picture of my past: @anna holding up a grilled cheese sandwich at the grand opening of LA's latest gastropub; @anna seated at a kitschy diner behind the highest stack of pancakes, sugar dusted; @anna dressed in silver at a Vegas steakhouse, cutting a massive ribeye, watching the juices pool; all meals I ordered, photographed, but didn't eat. A waste. A familiar fantasy, that I might return to the girl I was and consume what she did not. I would eat it all now, shameless. I would start a foodie feed, the upside-down version of the identity I constructed when I was a teenage girl, the alternate story. I see both grids, both girls, when I see @annawrey. I see stardom, what I chose, what became of me, and everything I missed.

I put down my phone, pick up the landline, press a button and listen to it ring.

"Room service closes at eleven, hon." The woman at the front desk has an awake voice. I tuck the pink receiver to my shoulder, check the time. I'm nine minutes late. "But the bar is probably still open," she says, and something about a limited menu.

I hang up, stand up, find those flip-flops. Hunting for food makes me brave. Or the pills have peaked and I'm less paranoid than euphoric. I unbolt the door, face the hallway.

8.

The day after the sex party, Jake and I slept into the afternoon. When we woke, I offered to go home. I liked the idea of solitude, the shower I'd take, Cup O' Noodles and Netflix, and no man there to judge what I consumed. But Jake said, "Stay," so I did. I wore his sweats, ate the salad he ordered me. We spooned on the couch and drank cans of La Croix laced with molly. He knew about the comments my mother had left on my posts; I told him about her phone calls and texts.

"She's sick," I said. "She has been for a long time." I heard my voice, sad, and tried to make it even. I missed her. And talking about her felt like a betrayal. How to explain: after the cancer had been cut out, healed, after the opioids had been kicked, after my father left, she had still been struck with a vague, recurring pain that seemed to move, according to her mood, from her feet to her forehead to her low back and tummy. But no doctor could locate the source. They said it was mental, suggested antidepressants and benzodiazepines she couldn't afford and was afraid to take, anyway. "I'm an addictive personality," she always said. "I prefer to depend solely on myself." Most of the time, I tuned her out, just like the doctors did. Because, in truth, I felt that I was the one she depended on. I was the one who bore witness to her pain, always hopeful when it dissipated, always disappointed when it returned. It was a burden, to listen to her complaints and try to fix them. It was a burden, to try and fix her. To stop her eating too many diet ice cream sandwiches, drinking too much Diet Coke and Yellow Tail. "Next time you see me go back for seconds," she always said, "you tell me to s-t-o-p." I did but she never listened. Usually, her gluttony was funny, anyway. Only sometimes was it sad, my buzzed mother diagnosing herself with an *addictive personality*, as if it were a crime. *Everything hurt* on nights like those, and I never said the right thing to make her pain stop. Usually, I just turned on the TV. Her favorite show, *The Real Housewives*, her favorite city, Beverly Hills, because, she said, "those gals are actually loaded." For years we had watched together, rapt. Lately, though, the drama had become rote. Or our phones had taken over, forcing us to scroll while the housewives fought, our eyes on our screens instead of the women. My mom liked to google their ages as she watched. She liked to google whether or not they were fighting in real life, and whether or not they knew the difference anymore. She was invested in people's stories. *The Hero's Journey* was how she saw her own. And mine. Also, she was sick. Other people rarely understood how she could be so many things, all at once. It was like they wanted her reduced, simplified.

"I'll call your mom," Jake said and wrapped his legs around my waist. "She just needs to know you're taken care of."

"She just needs to calm the fuck down."

"Moms love me. One heart to heart and she'll understand."

"I'll handle her," I said and disentangled myself.

I went into the master bathroom, sat on Jake's damp bathmat and cued up my mother's number, then navigated away, checked Leah's Instagram. Her latest post was an image of the ocean: glassy blue and a sinking sun. I double clicked to like it, my heart the only heart. I couldn't tell if it was the molly, or the sex party, or just the thought of Leah, but I felt woven into the world, no separation. I commented, "call me." It was the same thing my mother had written in her last text. I opened the message—*call me*—and pressed her number. The phone rang and I told myself to be patient, I told myself to be kind. Often, I went into conversations with this goal and failed to keep it. "How can *everything* hurt?" I would say, certain I understood my mother's pain, its limitations. Or scared because I couldn't understand. But once I made it as a model, an influencer, I'd send money home to her, tell her to see a therapist, or whatever specialist she felt she needed, or buy whatever supplement she'd heard might help. Finally, I'd be able to fix her. Even if I thought I shouldn't have to.

The phone rang three times before Jake's knock shook the bathroom door and I hung up. The door opened.

"You okay?" he asked. I felt my face go warm. I could have been taking a shit.

"Yeah," I said and stood. He moved closer. His pupils were pits and they swallowed his face up.

"I just got an email about you," he said.

It was my mom, I was sure of it.

"For a job," he said. "This big cannabis company—Blaze?" I covered my mouth with my hand.

"Promotional parties and socials, if things go good maybe billboards."

"Omg!" I yelled into my palm. Jake was dressed in black, but he looked shimmery, soft. I took my hand away and we kissed. Then he turned me to face the mirror and hugged me from behind, his arms around my waist like we were posing for a prom picture.

"There's a few details to iron out," he said to our reflection.

I said yes, anything, full of safe, sweet oxytocin, that celibate love everyone talks about when they talk about MDMA.

"Like, have you ever considered getting implants?"

I wasn't sure what he meant. I was smiling when I said, "What?"

He said, "Breast implants," and his voice was quick and sweet, the same voice someone else might use to tell me I had spinach between my teeth, a new mole on my back.

"Blaze is generally looking for girls with a curvier ascetic." He stared at me in the glass. "And I was thinking implants might help you move to the next, like, phase of your career anyway."

I blinked, saw spinning behind my eyelids. As if I had sugar binged and was suffering the aftermath, the crash, the mortifying flush of blood to my face, suddenly red and warm and ugly. I told myself to look at Jake, but couldn't, and turned my gaze to the floor. "I can't believe you're asking me this," was all I could think to say. No, I had never considered getting implants. Lean like the models I'd grown up looking at, that was how I'd fashioned myself. When it came to Instagram, selling anything, I'd thought a body that promised absence— of hunger, of desire itself—was worth more than flesh. I hadn't noticed the ideals were changing, or that they'd been made up to begin with. I knew—from Instagram memes, mostly—that top surgery was noble, a worthy, gender-affirming transformation, knew post-mastectomy reconstruction was also. But a boob job was silly and embarrassing, a job for silly embarrassing women, porn actresses, Real Housewives, Pam Anderson. Girls like me didn't get breast implants. We didn't need to be affirmed, or weren't supposed to.

"Babe." Jake latched his arms tighter. "It's no big deal, an outpatient procedure, like thirty minutes and it's over. I know tons of girls who've had it done." Tons of girls. On his account, in his DMs. "I mean, I don't care, I think you're beautiful, but for this level of exposure—" He turned me to face him, lifted my chin and made me meet his eyes. "Just think about it," he said.

I nodded yes but my mouth was closed. When he kissed me, I kept it shut. Because what had he said about the IUD? *So easy.* And inserting it had hurt more than he understood, more than I suspected he'd ever have to understand. He pushed his tongue into my mouth and I let him. He fucked me before the mirror like our reflection was the cure for whatever I was feeling. I felt self-conscious, yes, my small B-cup breasts too small now, the plate of bone between them protective as armor, and just as repellent. Also I felt fear. I might have felt rage and beneath it a sorrow tall and wide as a man's leaving body. But by the time Jake finished, pulling out from inside me and coming on my sacrum, I felt nothing. At least I thought so.

But afterward, I couldn't sleep. Jake bumped ketamine to kill the molly and pass out and I stayed up, propped in bed beside him, searching: paid placements for plastic surgeons; before and after photographs of headless breasts; assurances of rapid recovery augmentations, patented incision techniques. And an advice column on a feminist website titled *Help! My boyfriend wants me to get boob implants*, the letter writer identified only as Itty Bitty Titties.

"I've never loved my breasts," Itty Bitty Titties wrote, "and this is the father of my child! And now that he's admitted he wants this, I sort of do, too. But I also want to raise my daughter to feel good about herself. What do I do?" DUMP HIS ASS was the only sentence of the columnist's response. But I couldn't dump Jake's ass, not when I was so close to actual work, stardom, money.

I opened Instagram, found Blaze Cannabis. The grid was all images of tastefully lit THC cartridges and flowers, ad campaigns of busty brunettes with impossible waists watering pot plants. *Sweet Greens* and *Bodacious Buds* the captions read. Below it, the Blaze logo, a neon-headed panther, bore its teeth. I touched the post. The name of the company owner, Blaze Balzani, showed as tagged. I touched it.

Blaze the man had nine million followers. They left lengthy comments on his posts, called him "KING OF BROS" and "Rey 👑👑👑" and requested his help like he was an actual king: "Please sir, I must leave my country and come to America to live as you do please I beg you to send assistance sir."

Sad. Especially because it was the women followers wanted, the women who showed them what to want. Blaze's personal feed, more than the feed for Blaze the brand, was full of them: Blazed Buddies in panther-head string bikinis, a uniform. Blaze himself seemed to have one too: swim trunks or shorts in ironic patterns. Panthers of course, but also Ninja Turtles, prison stripes, pink camo. Through Tulum and Vegas, Hawaii and Thailand he strode, short-shorted, flanked by a herd of augmented Buds. Buds in bubble baths, playing with the foam. Buds on pool floats. Buds on skis. Buds grilling sausages. Buds Jell-O wrestling, mud wrestling, wrestling with giant snakes that clung to their bodies like anxious children. I scrolled. Next to me Jake breathed, every exhale tacked with a sigh. *Dump his ass*, the columnist had advised Itty Bitty Titties. And what would my own mother say? I thought of a story she told about my dad: a year before I was born, dinner out, her birthday maybe, his eyes on his steak, silk napkin in her lap.

"This back pain is killing me," she said. "I want to have them reduced." She gestured at her chest. My father didn't look up from his plate. "And get rid of your best asset?" he asked. And that was when she knew he would someday leave her.

"I guess I need them now anyway," she said once he did. In one of my first memories, I sit on her bed and watch her rifle through her drawers for a push-up bra. So what would she say about surgery? *Oh honey, no.* And what would I have to say to reassure her? *My body, my choice.*

Jake rolled over. I closed my phone, my eyes. I waited for sleep that didn't come. I knew it didn't matter if Itty Bitty left her man or stayed. His words were fastened inside her now, implanted.

IN THE MORNING Ella texted, "Come with me to the med spaaa?" and I wrote back "Yessssss," eager for escape, girl time.

Her injector, Shonda, was powder-faced, her cheeks and lips like marzipan, technically edible but also artificial, too rich to chew. "Welcome to my world of beauty," Shonda said when we arrived. She led us to a treatment suite and Ella sat in a pistachio green recliner, feet dangling like a child, hands clutching the handle of a giant mirror Shonda passed her. I sat in a normal chair next to the door, phone in my lap, buzzing, checking, closing, opening.

"Okay babe, what are we doing today?" Shonda asked and Ella held up the mirror, stared at herself.

"I think I need more Botox here," Ella said, and pointed at the middle of her forehead.

"Correct," Shonda said, "your elevens need softening."

"And I think I need a lip refresh also."

"Move the mirror, let me see," Shonda said, and I could tell she was trying, but failing, to frown.

"Let's do one unit of Voluma filler and if as I inject it starts looking like too much for your lips, I'll place the rest of the syringe here." Shonda pointed at the faint lines hanging like curtains around Ella's mouth. Ella held up the mirror again. "I never noticed those," she said.

"Nasolabial folds," Shonda said. "Everyone has them, yours are just a little deeper than I like to see." She removed four syringes from a mini-fridge. I swiped open the camera on my phone, examined my own folds in selfie mode, nowhere near as deep as Ella's. Shonda stuck her head out the door and yelled, "Becky!" and an assistant came in and tapped Ella's forearm, "Just to, you know, take the focus off the pain a little."

Shonda injected Ella's forehead and the assistant tapped and talked about whose lips, chins, cheekbones she liked, and whose she didn't. "Personally, I think Kylie looks best with three syringes," she said. "It's when she goes for four that things get weird." I pulled up Kylie's Instagram, pinched to expand each picture. I thought she looked better with her lips maxed out, full to bursting. But I kept that to myself.

"Oh for sure," Shonda said. She switched syringes then jabbed a needle into Ella's top lip. I closed my phone to watch.

"I mean, everyone has at least a syringe in there at a time, and everyone's different, but I draw the line at five." She pulled the needle out, put it back in. Ella's eyes watered. Her lips went red and swollen.

"All set," Shonda said. "Good job, honey." She gave Ella a pink ice pack and turned to me. "Okay, Little Miss Anna, how about a consult?"

"Shonda is the injection queen," Ella said. She eased out of the chair, sat in a smaller seat beside me. I looked at the door, then at Shonda. Her face shone in strange places, like saran wrap, pulled tight.

"Just a consult," I said and moved to the recliner, stretched out my legs, tucked my phone between my thighs and squeezed it there. Shonda loomed over me.

"Okay, frown," she said and I frowned. "You have hyper-expression here," she pointed at my hairline. "And here," she touched my third eye.

"It's extreme for someone so young, and it'll only get worse with time." She put a gloved hand on my shoulder and I felt it, the problem of time, the solution; the care of women, the comfort.

"I suggest twenty units of Botox," Shonda said, "the standard preventative dose."

"Yes," I said.

"Boto party," Ella said and clapped her hands.

"Alexa," Shonda yelled, "play Ariana Grande."

"Playing Ariana Grande," a robotic woman's voice replied.

Becky tapped my arm and Shonda told me to relax. She inserted a needle into my forehead, took it out, put it in again, miniscule jabs along my hairline. They stung, made sounds like snapping, followed by spurts. Between my legs, my phone buzzed and I focused on the feeling of excitement, distraction.

"This is going to look so good," Ella said from inside the screen she was tapping. Shonda handed me the hand mirror. She got close, watched me watch the glass. I looked for a difference I didn't see.

"Hey, hon?" Shonda said, her voice lifted at the ends. "Has anyone ever told you that your lips are asymmetrical?" She pointed to the cupid's bow of my mouth.

"Huh," Ella said and put her phone down, craned her neck to look.

"No," I said. My grandmother's mouth, her smile. My mother always said that they belonged to me as well.

"I mean, up to you, but we could fill the top lip a little here," Shonda said, "and then even out the bottom here—it'd be so subtle. Like, one syringe of filler."

"It's safe, right?"

"Oh for sure, honey, it's just hyaluronic acid, your body makes it naturally." Shonda held up her hands. "Totally up to you."

Ella said, "I get filled every six months—so easy. Like getting your hair colored."

"If you don't like it, we can reverse it," Shonda said.

The room hummed. Ariana sang *greedy, I'm greedy, I'm*

greedy, I'm greedy. I felt my phone, hot against my thighs. A simple choice, a natural acid, and reversible if I decided I didn't mean to choose it.

Shonda said, "Filler gets a bad rap because when it's bad, it's really bad. But most people have it, you just can't see, you know?"

"Okay," I said, "one syringe."

The needle was small, but when it met my mouth, it spread pain through my face like a burn. "Perfect," Shonda said. She wiped the blood away, handed me an ice pack, a mirror. I looked to the glass and that's when I saw it: instant growth, instant healing, instant transformation. Like a drug, straight to the vein. And instantly, I wanted more.

I said, "What would happen if we put another syringe in?"

"Knew you'd love it," Ella said. "The swelling is the best part."

"For that reason, best to wait," Shonda said. "See what you think once the irritation goes down."

"Baby steps," she added. "Lips should be *built*, but slowly, not in a day. Like followers." I was disappointed to hear it, a little ashamed, as if everyone could tell my appetite was bottomless. But I said no problem and slid from the chair.

"Looks so good," Ella said as Shonda walked us to the lobby and took her place behind an iPad, fixed with a credit card swiper. I had somehow forgotten we had to pay. Hanging out with Jake made me forget the cost of things. Maybe Ella would pay for me. She forked a thick black credit card between her pointer and middle fingers, then passed it to Shonda but looked at me.

"You can always get more," she said, taking the card back. Shonda turned the iPad toward me. I owed $1,200. "I gave you our friends and family discount, Miss Anna," she said, and winked. I fumbled in my backpack for my debit card. I didn't have the money. But I handed the card to Shonda anyway and she swiped fast. The pad dinged and I looped my initials across the screen. Just like that, my account was overdrawn. I was entirely dependent upon Jake. I checked my phone for his name, the bubble of a text, saw only a missed call from my mom. I cleared the notification, locked the screen, and followed Ella out the door.

SHONDA'S OFFICE HAD been pink-lit, cast in a womblike glow. On the street, the sun harshed everything. We walked Roxbury Drive, ice packs pressed to our mouths, and Ella flipped her phone, filmed herself, swollen, wet with melt.

I said, "You share this?"

She lowered the phone. "Why not?"

"I guess I thought it'd be a bigger deal than it is," I said.

"I felt that way before I got implants."

"Wait, what?" I told her about Jake, what he'd said.

She rolled her shoulders back, shimmied her chest. "Mine are big Brazilian B-cups," she said. "I had like, mosquito bites before. My followers grew after I healed, though obviously I don't tell them about things like *surgery*, that's TMI." She looked at her reflection in the phone again. "If you admit to doing little tweaks like filler or whatever, everyone will believe you when you're like, 'I didn't get implants, I just gained weight.'"

"Did it hurt?" I asked.

"It was rapid recovery. Literally I went in at 9 *a.m.*, home by noon, and then I just lay around popping pain pills and eating, it was the best. I was at the Grove buying new tops two days later."

I considered my own B-cups, how slight a change I'd have to make, how small a surgery. I considered my followers, the continual transformation required to nurture their attention, make it grow. I considered the journeys I'd seen on other people's stories. Fitness journeys, wedding journeys, weight loss journeys. Journeys into marriage, motherhood. Journeying was my job now, not personal, just work. I opened my phone, took a selfie shaped like a kiss. Before I edited and posted, I searched @Naurene48, and blocked her.

"NOTICE ANYTHING DIFFERENT about me?" I asked when I returned to Jake.

He looked me up and down. "You're hydrated," he said.

"Nothing else?"

He shook his head, touched my nose, called me cute. *So subtle*, Shonda had promised. And she'd been right. That night I slept on my back to keep the toxin from pooling. In the morning I woke, ready for more. More of the change, the instant growth I'd seen when I looked in the mirror and met my swollen mouth, new smile. I hadn't known it was so easy to fill up, hydrate. If other women knew how easy it was, they'd all do it. Why didn't they know? I asked Jake and he shrugged. Women were always looking to tear each other down, he said. "No offense, but y'all like, don't want each other to be hot." I wanted to be hot. And fuck other women if they couldn't support my choice to be hot. I told Jake I was "boob job curious," and he furrowed his face and said, "You sure?" like he was concerned, like it hadn't been his idea in the first place. "I'm curious," I said, and he made a call, a receptionist squeezed us in. We sat side by side in a room made for keeping wealthy people waiting. A white baby grand piano and crystal chandelier. On the coffee table by our knees, a scented candle and several binders of photographs—evidence of Dr. Marilyn Holle's impressive work—A-cups to C-cups, double chins to single chins, hooked noses to smooth, upturned buttons. On the wall, a framed *90210 Magazine*, Dr. Holle on the cover, a stethoscope around her neck. The words, "Beverly Hills' Best Plastic Surgeons" laced with her long, windblown hair.

"Anna?" The sound of my name called me out of the image, back to the room, then to the frame of a door that led me further back. Down a long hall of treatment suites, each door affixed with a gold number, a crystal knob. I followed Karen, Dr. Holle's nurse, watching the neatly trimmed ends of her flat-ironed hair sway against the back of her pink scrubs. Jake followed me, texting. We passed other nurses, all women, who turned and smiled. Here they were, the women who supported other women, #sisterhood. I had found them.

In a suite marked *Number* 7, I changed into a robe, then sat on an exam chair. Jake sat in a smaller chair, eyes on his screen. Karen the nurse took notes about my medical history on a pink clipboard.

"Alright honey, ever had surgery before?"

"No."

"History of diabetes, heart attack, stroke?"

"No."

"Cancer?"

"Not personally."

She took photos of my body in front of a blue screen—"A little to the left, hon, okay good, now turn to face me? Perfect"—shooting my breasts at every angle. "You're an excellent candidate," she said when she was finished. Who isn't? I wondered but didn't ask. Addicts, maybe, women who came in already implanted, already filled, and still wanting more.

"Dr. Holle will take good care of you," Karen said as she left the room, her voice low like she was divulging a secret I should feel good about. And I did feel good. I felt relieved to be taken care of, an excellent candidate.

Dr. Holle knocked, then entered. In the flesh she looked the same as her photograph: Photoshopped. She looked like she'd be cold to the touch. Jake stood and shook her hand. "Good to see you again," they said to each other. Dr. Holle sat on a rolling stool and checked her chart. "So what brings you in today, Anna?"

"Okay," I said. My voice belonged to someone else. I fumbled with my phone. Just this morning I'd filled my notes app with questions. The internet had advised prospective patients to ask lots of questions. "I have some questions," I said but Jake cut me off.

"Excuse me, ladies," he said, "I'm going to step out and take this." His phone wasn't vibrating. I waited for the door to close behind him, glad when he was gone. Because I wanted what Dr. Holle had the power to give me and didn't want Jake weighing in like it had been his idea. The internet had told me plastic surgeons wouldn't operate on women who came in at their boyfriends' or manager's or boyfriend/manager's behest. "Dump his ass!" they'd supposedly cry.

"I know breast implants are a safe, common procedure, and I'd like to have them done," I said. "I would like to know what kind of incision you recommend and what size—I'm thinking a full C-cup. And I would like to know whether you use textured or smooth implants and your opinion on the Keller Funnel technique."

Dr. Holle smiled at me like I was little, a little girl. "Okay honey, let's see what we're working with first." She drew my robe open, surveilled my torso like an empty canvas. I smelled her coffee breath. She squeezed each breast with a force that surprised me, coming from a woman. Her fingers were actually cold. When she let go she rolled backward on her chair, turned to a computer, and started typing. "I'm going to issue a diagnosis of hypomastia with slight asymmetry."

"Hypomastia?"

"It means not enough breast tissue. And your right breast is slightly larger than your left."

"Right," I said like I'd always known that when in truth, I'd never noticed. So many things about myself I hadn't noticed. When I looked in the mirror, I apparently didn't see what other people saw.

"You're an excellent candidate for silicone implants," Dr. Holle said. "Given your low BMI, I recommend no more than 450 cc, smooth, moderate profile, delivered via a periareolar incision. Anything bigger would look out of place on such a small girl."

She smiled and I smiled back.

"Any questions?" she asked.

I had so many. "Not that I can think of," I said. I hadn't known I was too small or asymmetrical, and now I did. The truth was a comfort when I knew how to fix it.

"Alrighty," she said. "Karen will take care of you." She left just as Jake came back. Karen came next and led us to a room with a desk and a computer. She passed me a printed-out sheet of prices. Certain brands of implants were more expensive than others. Jake took the sheet, passed it back. He removed a credit card from his back pocket and paid $9,000 in fees to secure a surgery in four days' time. He said the cheaper implants were fine for my "first set." He said I could get him back when I confirmed the Blaze Cannabis job, became a Blazed Bud, became famous. He said I could live with him at least until then. "We'll see how it goes," he said and I thought of my mother, how I'd get famous and send her a check like a good daughter, a whole, perfected daughter. Once I was fixed, I'd be better all around.

TOGETHER, JAKE AND I went to a lab and had my blood drawn, then to the Airbnb to clean out my stuff. We went next to Target. Aisles opened up for me in every color, a packaged, painted landscape: tubs of a protein powder called Fit Girl with 110 calories per serving; and sixty calorie pudding cups and zero calorie Gatorade and extra strength Tylenol and laxative tea; sports bras with front closures, and wet wipes and scar gel. I piled it all, like the rest of my stuff, in a corner of Jake's walk-in closet.

That night, sleepless again, I lay in bed and sifted through the comments on my latest post—

@coomelapapi: #GOALS
@vfgallardo1790: Te amo
@animerulz202: Are you OK
@lyfeof_myah: @jelianna did she get her lips done?
@ansh.singh.man7311: love you
@hoola_party: 🎷👍more pleaseeeee

—I sifted through my DMs, turning lately, as my following grew, toward violence. *You disgust me. Cunt. Ima turn that ass inside out. Choke on this cock. Make you bleed.* One by one, I blocked the senders. I looked for Leah's name among them. It wasn't there.

On a website called TrueYou.com, I read blogs written by women on day one after breast augmentation, day two, day fourteen. "Finally myself," they said and, "Why did I wait so long?" The comments on their posts were all from other women. "So proud of you," they said, "so happy for you," and, "sending so much love your way." I clicked the profiles of those who commented the most, saw lists of the surgeries each woman had chosen, lived through, the blogs they'd written about how they'd healed and what they wanted next. It was apparently commonplace to undergo multiple cosmetic procedures on the way to wholeness, selfhood. Some women even set out timetables for their entire body transformation, order of procedures, wish lists of surgeons, lines of credit. Were these women addicts? Or were they simply empowered, in touch with their desire, financially and spiritually ready to pursue the body of their dreams, the shape in which they'd finally feel at home? Home might take a lifetime to achieve, but these were women #blessed to have money or good credit, a healthy baseline to begin with, a whole lifetime to give over to achievement.

Achieve, a word used often on TrueYou.com. *I've achieved the breasts, flat tummy, and butt of my dreams!* Now on to the neck and lower face. Maybe also a rhinoplasty, lip implant. With an endoscopic brow lift, might as well get an upper blepharoplasty, too. An upper blepharoplasty was not, as I'd previously thought, a surgery reserved for Asian eyes only. TrueYou.com pointed this out; an upper blepharoplasty was a procedure for *hooded* eyes, which anyone could have. And yet, most of the TrueYou.com blepharoplasty reviews I scrolled were written by women complaining of their natural Asian eyes, their "natural squinty eyes," that had made them uncomfortable for far too long. "All my life I've been teased about my eyes," one woman wrote, "and now, finally, I feel awake."

I toggled between her before and after photos. "Day one and I'm already thrilled with my open, brighter expression," she wrote, and what sort of woman would I be if I wasn't thrilled for her?

MORNING OF MY own Day One: I gave Jake my phone to keep safe. I left him in the waiting room. In suite *Number* 7 I put on a cotton gown, a shower cap, socks. Karen came for me, had me pee in a cup, then walk myself into the operating theater, lie myself down on a metal table. She covered me in a blanket. Dr. Holle appeared. Together, we counted. Thirty, twenty-nine, twenty-eight, twenty-seven . . . My last thought before I drifted off was whether I would wake. My last thought was of my mother, how I hadn't bothered to say goodbye. Then, all thoughts ended and there was only darkness, deep space without time, without pain.

I WOKE IN the passenger seat of Jake's Land Rover. My chest was thick, tight. I touched it, felt ace bandage, a mummy's protective swaddle. We were driving down Wilshire, the radio singing, *Dick so big it's like a foot is in your mouth.* I opened my mouth. It was an undusted room. I swallowed. Outside, streetlights and headlights and neon lights blurred, a twisted color wheel.

"What if men could get penis implants?" I mumbled.

"They'd all do it," Jake said.

"One hundred percent." It hurt to talk. I closed my eyes.

When I woke again, we were parked. Jake was on my phone.

"She can't right now," he said.

On the other end, a voice was yelling. I heard the word *daughter*, then the sound of my own name. There was a light and I climbed toward it. I had somehow moved again, now to Jake's bed, the covers tucked around me, his hand on my blanketed thigh.

"Babe," he said, "wake up."

My nipples pulsed. I pictured Dr. Holle peeling them off like petals, sewing them back on.

"I need a pill," I said and drifted inside where everything still turned, tumbled me, a plastic figurine like the princess toys I played with in the bathtub as a girl: Ariel and Aurora, Jasmine and Belle. My mother kept them in a basket under the sink. They were immobile, their arms and legs bent in stiff postures, their feet covered by skirts and molded to thick pedestals. But I had loved them, had gifted them stories beyond true love's kiss and happily ever after, stories of adventure, journeys of their own. And when danger befell them, when bad men threatened harm, I had given my princesses the power to fight.

I opened my eyes. Jake was shaking my shoulder.

"I talked to your mom," he said, too loud. "There's something important we need to discuss."

9.

Downstairs at the Princess Hotel, the lobby is dead, no music even. I flip-flop to the bar, still wearing the robe from my room, nothing underneath. The outfit seemed acceptable before and now feels borderline unhinged, a flasher's trench. But the bar is almost empty and I'm flying high anyway, not anxious, just warm, washed in the soft mania of my drugs. A man at the far end watches a muted big screen. A young bartender unloads a steaming dishwasher.

"Be right with you," she says.

"I need a minute anyway," I say and prop up on the stool closest to the door, peruse a menu.

Down-bar, the man's gaze shifts. I feel it find me, and realize as I do that he's the same guy I saw poolside earlier, watching. I cross my legs and arrange the robe. The bartender slides me a finger bowl of pretzels. It's been sitting out, getting breathed on, but I start in anyway.

"We're out of buns," she says.

I say okay and chew my pretzels, keep my eyes on the menu's limitations: salad, soup, fries.

The man picks up his wine glass. I feel him move, feel him where he lands two stools away and swivel in his direction, take in his Patagonia zip-up and ugly out-doorsy shoes.

"Nice outfit," he says.

"I dress for comfort," I say and he laughs.

"Care for a drink?"

"Sure," I say and smile reflexively. I look at the bartender, who is looking at me. I shouldn't be drinking, not more, not tonight. "What he's having," I say and drop the smile.

The man presents his hand. "Henry," he says.

"Nice to meet you, Henry." We shake. My wine arrives, a sinister shade of red. The waitress slides a cutlery set across the counter.

"Cheers," Henry says. We touch glasses, drink. I notice scars and sunspots on his hands.

"What do you do, Henry?"

"I was in finance, retired seven years."

In music, film, art, business; the men I met with Jake, the men I dated after, were all "in" industries. I don't want to talk to Henry the way I talked to them.

"Now I'm a car guy," he says. "A collector. Vintage, European. Art pieces, really."

"I'm in cosmetics," I say, unprompted, and it feels like a challenge to what I imagine Henry thinks of me. Like, surprise, I can be a productive person too.

"I can see that," he says. I take a deep drink, the glass all the way over my nose. "I mean that as a compliment," he says and tips his drink in my direction. "Good job."

I swallow, smile, think about my former life, the accomplishment of a girl loved by thousands. I ask him why Burbank, this themed hotel, made for kids and parents.

"Long story," he says. "Funny story." I don't prod, he tells me anyway. "My daughter has these dogs, brachycephalic dogs, bulldogs, bad breathers. She's moving to New York." He sips, shakes his head. "The dogs can't fly, so I'm the schmuck who volunteers to come out here, watch them while the movers pack up, then drive them across the friggin' country."

"My mom was a dog sitter," I say, aware, all at once, of the wine, the pills, my bathrobe and bare legs, what kind of woman they brand me, what kind of message they send. "I love dogs."

"I'm a dog person, myself," he says. "Dogs are better than people, I always say." He takes a bigger sip. "Though my daughter's are out of control. They're upstairs now, tearing the room up, probably." We talk for a moment about discipline, then Los Angeles, his theory on California in general.

"Nanny state," he says.

"I'm from Texas," I say. "I know freedom."

"Lone Star Girl," he says and the air around us drops an inch, almost imperceptible. I meant to order food, but I'm no longer hungry. Because now is the moment. I chug, anticipate Henry's voice, telling me what he wants; telling me that what he wants *is me*. Yes, I want to hear him say it. He watches me drink, smiling over his teeth, like he knows what I can't know and always will.

"What?" I ask.

"Nothing." He shakes his head. "You remind me of someone."

"That never feels like a compliment," I say and wonder if he's remembered me, somehow—a decade younger, belonging to a younger, purer face—from some bygone Instagram search hole he fell down when he was younger, too. He starts in with a story about an ex-girlfriend and money, but I'm in my head, scrolling imaginary search terms: #young, #teen, #model. I picture myself, editing posts, picking hashtags, picture Henry minus the glasses and graying hair, thumbing his Explore feed, finding me in the black dress Jake bought me, the black block heel pumps I'd picked to match, finding me posed in the backyard of the sex party house in the Hollywood Hills. There's a Zen garden, sand raked in circles, a koi fish pool, stepping-stones over the water. And in the distance, Los Angeles itself, one hundred thousand pins of light.

"Lone Star," Henry says, "would you like to meet my dogs?" I wait for him to continue. "I'd be remiss not to ask," he says, and I feel my pulse pick up, each beat counting down the hours until Aesthetica™, anesthesia, a darkness I may not return from. Six A.M., six hours out, the only surgery Dr. Perrault will perform in a day. He's careful that way. And truth be told, there aren't many people willing to assume the risks Aesthetica™ entails.

"I hope I haven't offended," Henry says.

"No," I say, too fast. I reach into the pocket of my robe to remove my phone, and it's like my hands are hooked to wires, commanding them from above. "Let me show you something." I open Instagram, type Aesthetica™ into the Explore bar, where it's already a frequent search behind @annawrey. The grid loads, stacked with women. In one frame, a face so riddled by bad cosmetic work it's taken on the weighted, rubbery texture of a mask; in the next, the mask's natural double, the woman it was fashioned after, returned to normality, her normal natural beauty.

"What is it I'm looking at?" Henry says as I pass him the phone. He squints over the top of his glasses. Why does his opinion matter? All at once, it feels like a permission I must have, in order to get what I want. It feels like he's a husband, a father, a keeper of my freedom.

"I'm having a procedure in the morning," I say. "This one."

"But these people are sick," he says and pokes the before images.

"Yes, they were," I say, suddenly excited. "And now they're better." I reach over, swipe to the afters. "It's a groundbreaking procedure, the only one of its kind."

He clicks the informational video clip I've seen one hundred thousand times before. *Glow back in time to the authentic you. Look in the mirror and see your real self again.* I talk over it.

"They use 4D technology to scan patients' faces and see the past work they've had done."

Henry looks at me, an expression on his face. Wonderment,

maybe—technological advancement, science, men and their inventions—maybe horror.

"Then they go in surgically and reverse the old procedures, stretch the skin out and wrinkle it with lasers or whatever so like, by the end, your face is the face you would have had if you'd aged naturally."

His own face is grim as he passes back the phone. I take it.

"I've been through a lot," I say. "I've made mistakes. I need to do something for me, you know?" He doesn't answer, and I wonder if he can see what's fake, now that I've admitted I'm fake, the fine lines and early jowling I've tried to fill in and freeze, worsening everything in the process; the chin filler, extending like a pointed beak long beyond where my real bone ends; the outline of old silicone cheek implants; the tear trough filler that's made my eyes beady and small; the botched nose jobs and lip lift.

He reaches for his wine glass, drinks deep. I clear my throat.

"Six *a.m.*," I say. "I have to be there at six," but my breath is stuck and the words come out like whispers. I want him to ask me upstairs again, want him to tell me I don't need Aesthetica™, that I'm real the way I am, even if I won't believe him.

Henry puts his wine glass back with a clink.

"*Women*," he says, finally.

"What?" I say, braced.

"I prefer a natural look is all."

"That's what this is all about," I say. "Undoing the unnatural work you've had done in the past."

"You look great," he says.

"But this is all fake," I say and touch my face, thinking as I do of the mother from the pool, her body, how it looked to me like home and wholeness, the woman I want to be, the woman I could be, if only I hadn't tried for so long to stay a girl. I think of the little girl, the daughter—*Isabelle*—how her whole body craned in the direction of the hot tub, where older girls postured, preening to be seen. *Rhinoplasty, brow lift, buccal fat pad removal.*

"How much does something like this cost?" Henry asks.

"I need it," I say. "You don't understand." The property I borrowed against to be here, the debt I've taken on, the embarrassment of my vanity, the life I'm willing to risk. He can't understand it, and his refusal to even try, or to believe me when I tell him what I need, begins to give way to anger.

"You're a man," I say, "you can't understand. You all say you want natural, but what does that mean? It means the illusion of natural."

"Calm down, Lone Star," Henry says, but I'm off my stool, pulse racing, blood pushing me to act. My eyes dart to the cutlery, the knife's point. They dart to the door.

"You know what, fuck this," I say.

"Sit down," he says and kills his wine.

There's no safe way to reject a man. So I make a show of it, storm off. Henry talks in my wake, calls out a room number. But I don't look back.

THE LOBBY IS extra empty, the front desk unmanned. The elevator's there and waiting. I rush inside, hit the number for my floor. The doors don't shut and I tighten my robe, punch the close button. I'm sure Henry's arm is imminent, reaching out to wedge his body in. What am I capable of if he does? I ball my hands into fists. My nails dig into my palms, sharp enough to tear the skin. I punch the button again. The box gives a lurch, but the doors don't close. Behind my eyes I flash to a vision of Dr. Perrault, scalpel in hand, cutting, peeling, suturing the mold of my unaugmented face—an appropriate face for a woman my age—to the ravaged one I've made out of time and toxins and other, careless surgeries, the assurances of other careless men. So many misplaced wants, forgotten mistakes. Slowly, the doors ding shut and my whole body gives. The box rises. I open my Instagram, my messages. It's not too late to cancel Aesthetica™, lose the money I put down, keep the face I've made. It's not too late to speak.

The doors open next on my dark floor. Shaking with adrenaline, or hunger, I trip down the purple length of carpet, eyes on every door, every possible danger. Outside one, I see a disheveled room service tray—metal lid, empty cup. And beneath a tossed-off napkin, a serrated steak knife. I speed toward the blade, squat to grab it. While I'm down there, I lift the lid off the plate, see the sad aftermath of a child's chicken finger dinner—two half-chewed tenders, a smattering of soggy fries. I hesitate, scan up and down the hall. Then, I pick up the tray and carry it with me toward the Princess Suite.

10.

In this picture from the museum of my past, I am recovering from my breast augmentation in Jake's white-sheeted bed, in his white-walled condo, posting images from the shoots he organized, counting on the sponsorships he promised.

In this picture, I feel powerful in proximity to his power. In this picture, I feel small. In this picture, I want my mother and am afraid to want her.

In this picture, I am barely healed, only one-week post op but out of bed, at the airport. I scan the ticket Jake bought me, board a plane that takes me away from him. On the seatback screen in front of me a miniaturized 747 ticks toward Texas, my mother, like a clock.

"She's been trying to reach you about this," Jake had said, Day One of my new, augmented life. "She says she hasn't been able to get through."

It felt like an accusation, exposure. I was a neglectful daughter, and wrong for pursuing my own surgery, the perfection of my body, when my mother was trying to tell me hers had failed. Absorbed in @annawrey, I hadn't listened; I had ignored her calls. So it had been Jake who answered my phone, Jake she told about the pain in her gut, how it had worsened since I left. She'd gone for bloodwork, scans, all of which reported nothing. But she was certain they were wrong and had scheduled a surgery to find out why. An exploratory operation, invasive enough to necessitate my return, she promised. Though I wasn't sure I should believe her.

Out the airplane window, the sun rose. I filmed its purple, orange, yellow. I opened the purple, orange, yellow Instagram square, shared, then thumbed around my Explore feed. Since surgery, I'd deep-dived on a few weightlifters' boob job journeys, and now fitness content dominated my algorithm: videos of the squats, lunges, hip thrusts and protein calculations required to build six-pack abs and thick, lifted, 100 percent natty asses. But weights won't build breasts. And itty-bitty titties won't win body building belts. So, surgery was a necessary, personal choice to be shared, along with tips toward healing—eat clean and light and lots of protein, try not to stress about time off from the gym, sleep propped on pillows, drink extra water and try this electrolyte brand for added flavor, use code HYDRATE20 for 20 percent off— most of which, I followed.

The plane landed. I wheeled my suitcase, followed signs, other passengers. Into thick Texas heat, I emerged. I had acclimated to LA's embalmed air, the wind leached dry and dangerous. But humidity, Houston, my every gland, pore, hair follicle opened to absorb them.

AT THE TAXI stand I took off my backpack, my sweatshirt, which I tied around my waist. I put my bag back on, carried my phone, found my rideshare. A sedan, stinking of spruce air freshener, carried me up I-45 toward Texas Medical Center, the big hospital complex Houston is known for. It was the site of my mother's first cancer diagnosis, when I was too young to remember. But she had many times driven me past the long row of white buildings; she had many times pointed to one and said that was where they'd cured her, and where she'd first tasted the painkillers that made her sick in a different way. So, the hospital for her was both good and bad, proof she hadn't fabricated her pain, and the source of another, trickier pain, addiction being that much harder to excise.

Now, for me, the hospital felt like proof of my meanness, the callousness with which I had ignored her calls. But it also felt like a contrivance, the one place my mother could go to get my attention and summon me back to her. I told myself not to think of her that way. Yes, she was an addict, or had been once. But she wasn't dishonest, not by nature. She wasn't a bad mother. And anyway, Jake said that bad thoughts, bad vibes, had the potential to manifest bad realities. I decided to think only good thoughts, project only good vibes, and ignore the rest. I opened my phone, filmed myself smiling and lip-synching to the radio. *DJ Khaled, We da best MUSIC. 97.9 The BOX.* "I'm hooooome," I wrote in "strong" font, and shared. The driver turned into the hospital drop-off lot. I put my phone in my backpack, put my head down, focused on finding my way.

Visitor's desk and nametag, east elevators, sixth floor, surgery
suite. One attendant led me to another, to a nurse, who walked
me through a series of doors. She swiped her Employee ID
to expose the set of a TV drama, only badly lit, no gorgeous
people anywhere. We stopped at a curtained chamber. The
nurse said, "Knock knock," and drew the fabric back. I wrestled my hoodie on, urgent with the arms, the bulk a tent for me
to hide in. I wanted my mother to see my new breasts, larger
than I'd expected, too large to miss. I couldn't let her see.

She sat on a gurney, still dressed for living. Clogs and
stretchy jeans. She was on her phone, but looked up, saw me,
and her face went from flushed to a poached shade of white.

The nurse said, "You're supposed to have changed, you have
plenty of help now," and left, closing the curtain behind her. I
pulled at the hoodie's hem. My mother didn't speak. I wanted
to go to her but didn't. If she was faking, I was angry. If not, I
was afraid. Either way, I wanted her to tell me how to be.

Her lips were little waves of skin, seamed together. The
seam parted.

"What happened to you?" she asked. "Your lips." She
touched her own.

"What happened to *you*," I said and went to the gurney. She
stood, took my body in her body.

"Baby," she said and for a moment, I wanted to stay always
in her arms, warm where I needed nothing. But I couldn't stay;
I knew I couldn't and tried to pull off first. "No," she said, and
held tighter. My breasts ached where they were hidden. She

squeezed, then took a sudden step back and it was strange, how she reached for me, almost violent, like a groping man, her hands to my chest.

"Is this a bra?" she asked.

"Excuse me," I said and jumped further away.

Her face went from startled to shamed and I wanted to both punish and console her.

"Thank you for coming," she said, formal. She looked at the johnny, shower cap and yellow compression socks beside her on the mattress. I remembered them from my surgery, too.

"Don't thank me." I sat in a chair by the curtain and she stood to change.

"I want to know about LA," she said. "That man."

"Manager," I said.

"Your manager," she said.

"Isn't there more important stuff going on?"

"Do me a favor." She turned her back toward me, pulled off her top. "Be mindful of how they treat the pain. I need you to tell them what happened before."

I said, "Okay," and wondered for an anxious beat if drugs were what she wanted. Was the surgery an excuse to have them, even as she pretended it was not?

"It's important," she said. "We'll discuss the rest of whatever's going on here when I'm out the other side." She said it like a threat, a promise. Then she bent to take off her jeans, and I noticed the winnow of her legs, her shrunken ass, and felt a deep, familiar fear. Of my helplessness, and hers. I thought of so many stories I'd grown up hearing, messages from the world, cautionary tales about unaccompanied women, women without men. Women walking and running along isolated paths; road tripping women, pulled over for a pee at the wrong truck stop. Women with lives, women who forgot there were conditions to how they should be lived. Stories like that always ended in death.

My mother folded her jeans, her blouse and bra, put the johnny on, removed her underwear, modest. I heard my admonishments: *you need a wax*; and hers, *we women need to air our gardens out*. A new nurse parted the curtain.

"It's time," she said. My mother handed me her purse, her folded clothes, a list she had made of names to call when the surgery worked and she lived.

"I love you," I said. Maybe she told me she loved me too. But then she was gone.

IN THE ICU waiting room there was a beige phone. Sporadically, it rang. An old woman with a "Volunteer" lanyard around her neck put down her book to answer, announce a name and hand the receiver to the nervous respondent. One by one, they listened and left.

At the water fountain I swallowed Xanax, hydrocodone. Dr. Holle had prescribed them at six-hour intervals. But the pain cut through and I counted more, swallowed more.

Time passed, shortened by trips to the fountain, pills. Time passed in phone calls, good news of beloved bodies delivered from sickness to health. It passed in memes of animals doing human tasks, YouTube clips of precocious girls, lip synching Mariah Carey. It passed in Instagram stories: kettlebell swings, healing rituals, girls posed in cabanas with their current reads #selfcare. And Jake, jumping from a plane, parachuting toward green fields, whooping. I reacted with a 😵.

"Where are you?" I wrote and waited.

The sun set purple, orange, pink, before night warmed the room's fluorescence. The Volunteer packed her book and lunch Tupperware, removed her lanyard. "Good luck, honey," she said on her way out the door. I was alone.

There was a TV in the corner and I turned up the volume, changed the channel. *I never even looked at your husband*, screamed a woman on the screen. I took another Xanax. *With food*, the bottle instructed. I rifled through my mother's bag for cash, bought two bags of Cheez-Its from the vending machine. I ate, fast with the first, slower with the second, and felt myself transform, from empty to hungry, not full enough, still wanting. I eyed the vending machine, counted calories, checked Instagram. Ella had posted a new story in which she sat on a white couch, crying, her forehead so Botoxed it looked like laughter. But her eyes were wet, her mascara streaked, acne scars like braille, embossed into her skin. She hadn't used a filter and the texture of her face stunned me.

She listed symptoms. Brain fog, fatigue, insomnia and pain that shot in sparks through every muscle. "I've now been diagnosed with multiple chronic conditions," she said. "I've tried literally every treatment and nothing helps."

I sent a 👁🖤

"My DMs are open," she said, "if anyone has any ideas about what the problem really is."

I sent a 🙏.

Somewhere in the hospital, my mother was cleaved open, a man searching for danger inside her. I couldn't imagine him finding it. But if he did, I could tell Ella, suggest she elect to be cut open, too.

I went next to Leah's account. The latest picture was of a marathon finish line. "Came in fourth! 💪" the caption read. I liked the picture, composed a new DM. "I guess I know why you won't call me. I guess you think I ghosted you after you moved away or whatever. But this is an emergency. Naurene is in SURGERY and it might be serious." I pressed send. It felt strange to use my mother's name that way. *Naurene* sounded formal, but also like she could belong to Leah and me both. And I wanted Leah's attention. I wanted to divest my share of Naurene a little, to spread around the responsibility I felt for her pain, as if I was both the root cause and the cure.

But why was I responsible? Why did my mother see me as someone to confide in, depend on? Why did she talk endlessly of everything that hurt her? Her quest for self-knowledge, self-love, feminism, womanhood, wholeness, was so public and I, of all people, should have understood her exhibitionism. But I wanted a mother out of pain, which took her from me. I wanted a love, Leah, who would stay when pain returned, as it always would. The day we said goodbye, I had cried and Leah had not. Just kissed my cheek and left my body like a bell, struck and ringing. She'd always had trouble with feelings. She'd always used our alter egos to express herself. Even as a girl, she'd rarely cried. So she didn't intend abandonment, I knew that. But once she was gone, I changed the story anyway, made it familiar: I was needy, wrong, unwanted by her and anytime she texted or called, I didn't answer; to do so would be to confuse the lesson of my unlovability.

On the TV, *Real Housewives* bobbed across a phosphorescent lawn at someone's baby shower, or bridal shower, or divorce party. I watched them apologize, then fight, and imagined my mom, waving her wine glass and weighing in, always wanting the women to connect. I waited for the beige phone to ring, the device in my lap to pulse. The pills inside me turned the implants inside me into flesh and blood. The pills turned time invisible. Eventually, I slept.

IN DREAMS I was with Leah again, the last summer of our little girlhood, the last summer before Instagram, every night spent together. I was with my mother, forty-something and celibate, prone to leaning into the mirror, fingers at her temples, lifting, stretching. "What do you think," she would say, "just a little tuck?"

"No," Leah and I yelled. We wanted her as she was, creased and beautiful.

In amongst the dream's hallucinatory light, my mother packed a cooler with snack packs, Diet Cokes and purple grapes, and drove us to our spot in Galveston. Leah and I shared the backseat, as we always did, neither of us wanting to be too far apart. My mom complained she felt like a chauffeur. She put on her Shania Twain CD. *Man! I feel like a woman*, we all sang. On the beach, we spread towels on the hard-packed sand. My mom watched us girls in the water. We dove for pieces of fool's gold, tossed the stones and took turns chasing a glint barely visible against the oil sludge. Leah wore her pink bikini, I wore my purple, colors vibrant enough to flash like coral in the dirty Gulf.

Time disappeared. We were ocean, animals. Only the call of my mother's voice could pull us back. "Girls," she yelled, "don't make me come in there." She was standing, adjusting her giant sunhat, shaking towels, by the time we waded to shore.

It was ritual: the chase, the cool shade of evening that ended it, diluted blue before the black. My mother's voice. The stick of vinyl on my bare legs when I buckled into her stuffy Prius, the heat of Leah's body next to mine, humid air pulling through the open window as we drove home. Home where we were wanted. Home where we were warm. Home, a girl, a woman, a beige phone, ringing, waking me.

I stood to answer. My vision was murked in places, like I'd swum up into daylight, the hospital, the dank and empty chamber where I waited. "Hello?" I held the receiver away from my face. The voice on the other end belonged to a woman. "Is this . . ." it asked and said my name. I answered yes and waited for her to tell me what to do, where to go. "The surgeon is on his way to discuss your mother with you," she said, and hung up.

I returned to my chair, my phone, and checked the screen to see the time, almost midnight. The door opened and a man came in. I blinked to focus. He was Jake's age, but taller. Blue-scrubbed, he towered over me, smelling like Purell and rubbing his palms. I reached up to shake his hand, but he kept his pressed together, kept rubbing.

"So initially we operated with an exploratory goal," he said.

I said, "Right," and realized I expected him to tell me there had been no point. I expected him to complain about my mother, her persistent search for problems that had no source. I expected a bill, endless zeros, the cost of her pain.

"I can't say why the CT scan didn't show it," he said. "But when I opened her, I found a total of three visible tumors in areas around the intestine, as well as the intestinal lining." He added, "I did my best to clear them out."

I heard myself say, "What?"

"We're changing the prognosis here a little," the surgeon said.

I said, "Okay," but it came out like a cough and I cleared my throat.

"I'll keep her in ICU for a few days, see how she does." His palms became a steeple he lifted to his mouth. "Then we discuss chemotherapy." In my hand, my phone buzzed. I swallowed over the clump in my throat, the same feeling I got when my mom called and I knew it would be a fight. It buzzed again and I looked. It was Leah.

"In the meantime," the surgeon said, "let's get you in to see her."

I nodded, lowered the phone, grateful the conversation was over and I could stop trying to respond the right way.

A nurse arrived and led me down a new tunnel of parted curtains, the bodies behind them in postures of violent repose. Flayed skin and vomit. A dull moaning. My mother, yellow as an Easter egg forgotten in a jar of dye. She had a breathing tube and it forced her face into her neck. I wondered what I had looked like when I woke from anesthesia.

"She'll be unconscious for a while," the nurse said.

"How long is a while?" I asked. "I have her stuff." I lifted my mother's giant turquoise bag, conscious of my hand shaking from the pills I'd taken or from the sight of my mother's body, I wasn't sure which.

"You hold on to that. She won't be up until tomorrow." The nurse fussed with my mother's tube. "No sense sticking around."

"She wanted me to tell you she has a history with addiction," I said. "Painkillers, a long time ago."

"Well, she needs medicine," the nurse said, eyes on the tube. "There's no way she can take the pain without it."

"She just wanted me to tell you."

"I'll look at her chart."

It was my cue to go but I lingered in the doorway. I wanted to be asked in. I wanted to get close. I wanted the nurse to talk to me gently, as she would a child. It's a feeling I still have sometimes, around women.

11.

Back safe in the Princess Suite, locked behind the deadbolt. I put the room service tray on the bed, take the robe off, toss it in a corner like it's dirty. Henry's wine kicked my pills up a notch and now everything is doubled.

I slide under the sheets and focus on the TV, the chefs inside it. Each person is two people, now. They offer up meals inspired by childhood memories. *Salt, acid, heat,* twin judges say. *Inedible,* they tell the loser. "At least I'm going out on a dish I believe in," she says. I check the time—11:47 P.M.—then reach for the room service tray I stole from the hallway. Carefully, with reverence, I remove the steak knife, place it on the bedside table. Then, I open the metal dish-cover to reveal cold fries and bits of chicken strips stained with ketchup.

They only make me hungrier. I should have ordered food, let Henry pay, let him watch me cut tough bites of meat, sop up the blood, chew, swallow, satisfy myself. And then? I could have stayed, let him lecture me about what I need or don't need, what's beautiful, what's true. I could have replied to *Vanity Fair,* could still. I reach for my phone. The TV plays a commercial for foundation. *Invisible*, the voice says, *effortless*. Maybe she's born with it. Maybe she's a natural beauty, an untouched beauty. The sales pitch for every powder, cream, procedure. But there's always a consequence, some side effect that keeps away the promised miracle. Acne from pore-clogging foundation. Asymmetry from filler injected willy-nilly. Body dysmorphia from the asymmetry caused by the filler, which even when dissolved leaves your skin stretched out and floppy. It's the same with pills: Vicodin cuts the pain, but then you can't shit; Ambien puts you down, but the nightmares make you want to stay up; Ativan helps you forget your anxiety but takes with it everything else you wanted to remember. I drop the phone. How can I trust my memory? My story, altered by time and drugs and every passage I've made into anesthesia, and out again. Even if I spoke to *Vanity Fair*, came forward about Jake, I've little reason to think the world would believe a woman like me, so obviously dysmorphic, out of touch with what's real. And if they did, there's always a consequence.

I push away the tray, pull up the covers. I'm feeling feverish. Because of the food, contaminated by some kid's grimy fingers? Or is it a deep feminine intuition, telling me not to go through with Aesthetica™ tomorrow? Maybe I should just commit myself to a mirrorless existence. I reach for my phone again, lift it to scan my retina and unlock the screen; I don't bother using face recognition, it never works for me. I navigate to my favorite contacts. There's only one name there and I press it, put the receiver to my ear. I listen to the crackle sound as the connection reaches over distance, time zones. Then there's a ring, two rings, three. Four rings and her voice picks up, Australian accent apparent as ever.

"Hi," the voice says.

"Hey," I say, surprised to have caught her.

"You've reached the voicemail—" I feel stupid and stoned and hang up, open Instagram.

I know what I'm doing as I do it. The thing I tell myself never to do, I am doing now. Explore page, search bar, "Jake Alton." I type the name and watch him load.

Searching Jake this way is like falling down a K-hole. It's like trying to move your body when you're drugged, paralyzed. It's like he knows I'm watching him and worse than thinking me pathetic, ugly, old, botched, he can't remember who I am.

But Jake, too, is unrecognizable. A salt and pepper Santa Monica dad for six years now, he hosts a YouTube show called Primal Life™, and has curated his Instagram (grown to three million) to match it. On his grid, he poses in front of handmade yurts, constructed on solo hunting trips to the world's wildest locales; he posts go-pro footage of himself stalking prey, felling moose, deer, and once, a small black bear, all with only his bow and arrow. He skins the bodies, eats the meat to survive, smokes the rest and brings it back to his family. Providing this way is essential, he tells his followers in the heart-to-heart stories he uploads once he's back on the grid. "It's primal," he says, part of men's instinctual truth, too often stifled by PC culture, the domestic sphere.

Maybe he's right—men do seem desperate for escape. But I hate watching him escape, hate his smug, self-righteous assurances of what's essential for living fully and well. I hate his cute kids and young—but not too young—wife, hate his entire rebranded life. I click his story, confident in the anonymity of my fake account: Jake at an outdoor gym, flipping giant tires; Jake in the backyard of his renovated craftsman, roughhousing with his twin boys; a sped-up clip of a woman's hands, tossing a summer salad in a wooden bowl; and a sponsored series at a hotel pool, tagged by a GIF that says *staycation* and the name of a nearby resort. I click through videos: Jake's twins wearing inflatable swimmies and splashing; Jake's wife in a sunhat, sipping a mimosa; and Jake himself, selfie mode, his wet hair dripping, his lips pursed and serious. I try to pinch the screen and zoom in to see him close, as if his face will prove he hasn't changed. But the story feature won't let me and then the story ends. I shut the phone, close my eyes.

When I open them, it's 5 A.M. and the alarm is screaming. Light cleaves the blinds and the TV tells a new story, the words *Reunion Episode* in outrageous font at the bottom of the screen. I must have slept. Soon I'll sleep again. Anesthesia, the purest rest from which I'll wake, reborn. Or I won't. I am numb, ready. I gather my phone, my wallet, zip myself into a sweatshirt and leave for the Aesthetica Center, where Dr. Perrault waits to return me to myself.

12.

The ICU bathroom was single-use, strewn with seat covers and toilet paper. I stood at the sink, opened Leah's message: "I'm running a race in Oregon this weekend. I'll change my ticket, come a night early, see Naurene."

I wrote, "you run professionally now?" and thumbed through sleeping arrangements in my head. Leah's back against my back. Her breath, rising and falling, a rhythm I could hang on to.

"What's wrong with her?" she replied. I let my fingers hover. Better to tell Leah the truth in person, I decided. I didn't want her to be alone with the news. "Still waiting on results," I wrote. As I pressed send, the image of my mother's body, small and yellow and alone, flashed across my mind. I put my phone on the sink edge, turned the water on, ran it cold over my wrists and imagined bending over the toilet, purging the pills I'd swallowed. I imagined falling to my knees at my mother's bedside, felled by the sight of her, helpless and far. This is what the movie version of me would do, unable to contain grief and terror of such magnitude. For years my mom had been certain there was something wrong inside her. And it had been up to her alone to save herself, to demand the surgery no one, including me, believed she needed. Bad thoughts manifest bad realities, Jake said. Guilt, my mother always told me, was boring and therefore bad. But I felt it. I couldn't help it.

I left the tap on for privacy, dried my hands on my sweatshirt then lifted it to check my breasts, zipped into a front-closing sports bra. I hadn't measured them yet, but they seemed bigger than the C-cups I'd asked for. It didn't bother me. If Dr. Holle had upped the size while I was unconscious, it was for the best. On TrueYou.com I'd read all about "boob greed," the phenomenon that sets in post operation, patients wishing they'd opted for bigger implants. I unzipped my bra just enough to see the bruises. They had changed, gone yellow since yesterday. I was healing, stronger than before. On YouTube I'd watched a man drive a pickup truck over a silicone implant to prove its strength. It rolled, tossed by the tires. But it didn't break.

My phone pinged. "I'll rideshare," Leah replied.

"It's easy to get you," I wrote, "send ur info when you have it."

I dropped my phone into my mother's purse, walked through the hospital with the weight of it on my shoulder, my backpack on my back. Twice I lost my way. Along with the list of names and phone numbers, my mother had given me directions to the location of her car. But I was still turned around, dwarfed by the diagnosis, the building, the heavy bag, and unable to drum up the courage to call my mother's list. Leaving for Los

Angeles had made me a source of pain, and her coworkers, her fellow NA group members, they all knew it. It felt foregone, that I would say the wrong thing and reveal how right she was to wish me better. Double doors parted. I passed into a warm corridor, then through another door, summer air like a wall when I met it.

My mother's ancient Prius was festooned with bumper stickers: generations of failed democratic candidates. *Nasty Woman*, read the latest. I touched the key, adjusted the seat. I took out my phone, checked for Jake, Leah, both inactive. Ella had a new story up and I sat there, watching her add ingredients to a blender. Layers of kale, banana, flax. "Fighting inflammation," she said and dumped a scoop of green powder over the mess. "Reishi mushroom, for anxiety." She pressed a switch to grind. With my free hand, I touched the car's start button. The air came on; stale coffee and Calvin Klein Euphoria rose up. The radio was off. My mother had driven to the surgery in silence.

I tried to count the hours since my last pill but couldn't decide if it was one or three. I wasn't sober, but it didn't matter. Houston, shaped like the rings of a tossed stone, was familiar enough. The hospital and my mother's home were both inside the smallest loop. I'd go slow, leave the radio off, take Montrose all the way. I put my phone on the seat beside me, facedown so I couldn't see it. At the exit gate, I gave the parking attendant my mother's credit card.

"You're supposed to use the machines by the elevators," she said. Her nails were long, like finger bones.

"Sorry," I said and she handed me back the card. "Sorry," I said again. She opened the gate. I drove through, onto an empty road, everyone still asleep in their normal lives.

I passed Rice University, and the edge of the Museum District, where oil barons dumped money into art. I passed the apartment in a prefab building on Richmond where my mother had moved us for a few forgotten months before her divorce settlement came through and she bought the cottage. It was a house that never flooded. No tropical storm or hurricane had touched even the cinderblocks it stood on. I pulled into the driveway and the car shuddered out a battery breath. Three months since I'd left, but it didn't feel like it. Los Angeles, Jake, the experiences I'd had there were sewed up inside me, separate from the stacks of bills and coupons, the recycling bin overflowing with cans of Diet Coke, the freezer full of Lean Cuisines and Smart Ones dinners I knew waited inside. I unlocked the front door, entered the house. Dissonance hummed inside me, a low thrum, the sound of the air conditioner when I pressed the button to start it.

I stood in front of the vent for a minute, then peed, filled a water glass and sat at the kitchen table with my phone and my mom's side by side on the tile surface. I checked my likes and requests and DMs as I listened to my mom's voicemails, eager well-wishers, promises to visit. I deleted them all, then moved to her computer and let my stories run while I wrote her list an email: *Cell service is bad in the hospital, but Naurene is on the mend!* As I had with Leah, I left out the tumors, the long recovery and chemotherapy the surgeon said was coming next. It felt like a protective measure, guarding other people from preemptive grief. For now, better to strike a reassuring tone, a tone to suggest that I was in control, fully competent, not avoidant or afraid. On my phone, influencers shared serums, teas, lists of favorite activewear, workwear, loungewear. I closed Instagram. The silence throbbed. The silence spoke, reminded me to post, to rejoin my virtual world, add my voice to the conversation, keep content at the top of followers' feeds, keep relevant. My mother had her community, I had mine, a gathering of fans I needed more than ever now. Only gone a day and I felt myself slipping, felt how easy it would be to simply fade away. Focusing on my platform was another protective measure. If I lost @annawrey, I would be one step closer to entirely alone.

But my body was unpresentable and I was high and tired. So I went the bookshelf, took out *Women Who Run with the Wolves*, *The Feminine Mystique*, *In Search of Our Mothers' Gardens*, my own mother's favorites. I stacked them on the table, angled the twisty lamp from her desk for light. I took a picture, cropped it close, no background. "Current reads! 📚🤓 #feminism," I wrote and posted to my story.

I watched the rotation for a while, then went to the kitchen and unsheathed one of my mother's Lean Cuisine chicken dinners from its plastic wrapping. The sauce simmered and snapped as the microwave twirled, cooked, beeped. I checked engagement while I ate. 500 views, 650 views, 700, *I love that book!* Followers wrote. *Yes, queen,* they said. *Show us your body,* they said. *Are you a manhater? Stupid feminazi* they called me. I flushed with their violence but tried to see it as a signifier of success. This is what Jake said: more exposure means more haters. "A growing pain," he called my trolls who felt, from this perspective, meager. Like there should be more of them. I left the worst on "seen" for a while before deleting. I took another painkiller and slipped into my mother's bed, placed my phone beneath her pillow, felt my brain slip under, too. Covers, blankets, drugs, all piled on and put me in the dark.

I WOKE IN the afternoon, groggy and dry mouthed. I sat at the table, called a number, then another, then waited on hold, listening to a voiceover advertise the hospital's services. *State of the art; Groundbreaking research; Largest Cancer Center in the World.*

"This is ICU," a woman's voice finally answered.

"I'd like to check on a patient," I said, and told the voice my mother's name. "I'm her daughter," I added.

The voice put me on hold again. *Excellence in patient out-reach. Innovative clinical trials.* "Still sleeping," she said when she returned, and I remembered my mother was drugged, too. She would be moved to a new floor in the afternoon. The voice gave me the room number. I wrote it down then went to the fridge and removed a Diet Coke from one of two long cardboard boxes. My mother bought Diet Coke by the case and drank several in a day, the way she ate low-fat ice cream sandwiches, her appetite excessive with the indulgences she deemed allowable, safe. I cracked the cap on my can, drank and felt the fizzy syrup hit my stomach, unhappy when it landed. Diet soda never sat well with me. But I often drank it anyway. I went to my bag, took out my pain pills, swallowed one and got in the shower. My mom had bought a new shampoo since I left, a brand I'd seen hocked on home shopping channels. I pumped out a handful, took too much. "You are not the only person in this house," she would say when I used up bath stuff, food stuff, Diet Coke, toilet paper, and didn't replace it. "Selfish behavior," she would say, then something about when she was my age. She was twelve when her mother died, and her father was a piece of work. She didn't have the luxury of adolescence, a childhood before pain. Maybe her pain meant my childhood was also tainted, though anytime I had the thought it felt like an excuse. Plenty of kids grow up without a dad. Plenty of kids have a sick parent they have to take care of.

Wet-headed, I slathered myself in my mother's body butter, dabbed her Euphoria on my pulse points. My nipples were taped with Steri-Strips I was supposed to let fall off on their own. One at a time, I peeled them away. Translucent stitches held me together. But they were the melting kind, and almost entirely absorbed. I took a burst of topless selfies, found the best one and filtered out the last bruised patches. I sent the image to Jake with a UU and a kiss emoji.

"Thinking about that cock," I wrote and touched the button to send. I closed the screen, feeling like it was smart, to remind Jake of my implants. It was important to stay relevant with him, too. I touched my hair, the new upside-down heart shape my breasts made over my sternum, covering the actual heart beneath the bone. I touched my phone again. Still nothing. What if Jake never responded? It seemed suddenly possible and I couldn't let that happen. The uncertainty of my mother's future made Jake's approval, his power, more important than ever. I needed money. I needed a plan. I couldn't imagine losing my mom. But I could imagine being entirely alone. I opened my photos, looked again at the image I'd sent. Moments ago it had seemed hot. But now it seemed tone-deaf, unstable. My mother was in the hospital. And here I was, showing off my fake tits.

I closed the phone again, tried to count breaths. Jake's reply, when it came, took only minutes. But it felt like longer.

"Thx for the pic, how's your mom?" he wrote.

I groaned out loud. "She's doing well, thanks for asking," I typed, unsure of how to tell the truth without overburdening him. Low maintenance, chill, that was the kind of girl guys wanted. Sick moms weren't sexy.

I waited for ellipsis to tell me Jake was typing. They didn't appear. I needed to change the subject, ask a question, something to keep the conversation going.

I wrote, "Where are you?"

"Belize for a few days."

"I miss u," I typed, then deleted it, gave myself the smallest props for deleting it, for controlling the need I felt building up in my fingertips, dangerous as any drug, prompting me to act before I carefully considered what to say, and how to say it. I put the phone down, focused on my breasts again, which I touched one at a time, with care. The weightlifter girls said massage was an important step in the healing, "fluffing" process. Jake had promised to do it for me. I squeezed a little, then let go quick. I kept thinking of that truck, speeding over a silicone pocket the size of a jellyfish. I kept thinking of how strong it was, the love sewn up inside me.

FROM THE DOORWAY of my mother's new room, I saw that she was awake. But her body looked unconscious, arms limp and noodled.

"Let's get you untangled," a nurse said. She leaned over the bed, parsed wires. "Okay?" she said and wedged a call button, a PCA bolus, within reach. My mom said, "Yes," and "Thank you," like a shy child, the words sing-songed and soft. I felt like the hidden witness of a private moment, but walked in anyway, swinging the turquoise purse too enthusiastically.

"I'm the daughter," I said.

"Hi," the nurse said. My mom stayed quiet.

"Hi, Mom," I said. "I brought your purse." She mouthed *hi* at me, then closed her eyes.

The nurse wrote her name—Nancy—on a whiteboard and asked for mine. She put "daughter," in parentheses.

"She's been through the wringer," Nancy said.

There were faces, happy to miserable, at the bottom of the board. She circled an expression of anguish. I rifled around in my mom's purse for my phone, which I'd dumped in there before leaving the house, along with two Diet Cokes, one of them for her.

"Have her use the button if she needs anything," Nancy said, and left.

I put down the purse, glanced at my mother. Her face was bloated, her eyelids thin and blue, as if her body had been dredged up from the bayou, where it had been dumped. That did happen sometimes. Quickly, I looked away. At my phone. My camera. I pointed the lens at the whiteboard, the faces, smiley to sad, then uploaded the image to Instagram. "Mood," I typed and added to my story. Beyond the bed a wide window looked out on Rice University, rows of live oaks, brick buildings, the cross-country track like a leather belt, buckled around nobody. Someone had arranged a powder-blue chemotherapy recliner to take in the view. I went to it, propped my phone upright on the sill. I pushed the chair close to the bed and felt the effort in my breasts, a sharp, pulling pain. I hadn't yet revealed them to my following. But before the surgery, Jake and I had planned a shoot: lunch at a Hollywood restaurant where Bella and Gigi had recently shot content of kale salads and turmeric tonics they posted to their feeds. I would order a burger, Jake said, sit in front of it and lift the hem of my top to show a hint of under boob. *Did she or didn't she?* followers would ask, and fill my comments with conjecture.

I looked at my mom, tucked in bed, covers tangled like a feverish child. Lightly, she snored. I unzipped my hoodie, beneath which I wore a sports bra, and my new breasts looked obvious from some angles, dubious from others. "You want people to wonder," Jake said when we planned the reveal. "But never really know."

I went to my phone, turned on selfie mode, video mode. I pressed the button to film and angled the recliner to see the screen. The shot caught my mom in the background, her sleeping face turned to the lens, showing both her sickness, and our likeness. For a moment I wondered if I should wait until she woke, ask her if she minded being broadcast to the world. But she was blocked from my account and would never know. I needed to do something; I couldn't just stand there, in the silence, watching my mother's waterlogged body work so hard to heal. I sat, crossed my legs, looked down at my breasts, then up at the red bead of the filming device.

"Hi everyone," I croaked. I cleared my throat, started again. "Hey guys, I just wanted to check in here and ask for your thoughts and prayers for my mom, who is recovering from cancer. She's a total warrior and with your good vibes, she's going to come through this stronger than ever." I heard her shift in bed behind me and turned. Her eyes were open. I looked down again but didn't bother to replace my hoodie.

"Hey," I said. She stared and I thought she might mention the video I was shooting, or my body, the shape of it. She looked, instead, at the wires plugged into her arm, the top of her hand. Almost horror, the expression on her face.

"Mom," I said.

"Some mistake," she murmured. "I'm not supposed to be here."

I glanced at the camera, the red bead still alive. Should I believe her? Was it the drugs speaking for her? I wasn't sure. What if there had truly been a mistake?

"Where are you supposed to be?" I asked.

"What?" Her mouth was full, every word in the way. I turned back toward her and spoke slow. "If you are not supposed to be here, where are you supposed to be?"

"Home," she mouthed, but didn't say.

"I brought you a Diet Coke," I said, removing the can and holding it, label out, for the camera. At home, when I had packed it, I'd imagined how grateful she would be for the treat, the thoughtfulness I was bringing to her care. I had felt useful, picturing myself delivering the soda to her, as if that singular act might fix her. But now she only nodded, blank-faced as I cracked the cap, handed her the can. She held it with both hands, lifted it to her mouth and slurped. I watched her, picturing the moment on film, a sweet, sharable version of our love I could shear away from her confusion, and offer to Instagram, the world. *Awwwww,* followers would respond. *Such a sweet daughter😇! Such a caring, loving girl.*

"That's good," my mother said and swallowed.

"Good," I said and imagined tagging @cocacola, imagined them reposting, sharing my account with a new audience, growing my followers from 60,000 to 100,000 with that short, simple gesture, winning me a blue check mark, verifying my personality, my account. It was possible.

My mother took another, longer sip, then handed me the can. I took it back, heard bubbles fizzing on the inside. She stilled and stared at the room in front of her.

"Mom?" I said. And that's when everything sped up. Her body in fast forward, pitched as if pulled. My body, rushing to help hers. Diet Coke-colored vomit, again and again, in waves. The paper towels I ran for, the button I pressed, once, twice, three times, four, to summon someone, anyone, to save us.

"DIET COKE, SERIOUSLY?" Nancy the nurse said when she hustled to my mother's side. She wore gloves, grabbed a wad of sopped towels, chucked them in a pink vomit pail.

"I didn't know," I said, and my own voice sounded like a whine, a buzz, the noise any device made to signal a call, a text, a notification of someone else's love. I looked to the windowsill where I'd left my phone, then back to Nancy, who was leaning over my mom.

"I'm so sorry," I said, and I meant it. But I was also stung. By my mother's weakness, by Nancy's clipped and critical tone.

"Let's get you clean," Nancy said, and started to work off my mom's soiled gown. I apologized again, but Nancy didn't answer.

I said, "It might help to know my mom has a history with pain medication."

Nancy still didn't look up. "I'll check her chart," she said.

"I have to go to the airport," I said. I had plenty of time

before Leah's flight landed but wanted to leave; I wanted Nancy to think I was competent, not mortified as I truly was. I added something about family flying in. Nancy should think my mom and I were supported, loved. But she didn't respond.

I went to my phone, stopped the video. I should keep this I thought. Jake had advised me to save any potential content. "You'd be surprised by what you can salvage with careful editing," he'd said. I turned my back to the room, faced the window and pressed play. On the screen I was small and so was my mom. I watched myself remove the can from her purse, crack the cap, pass it to her. There was a long, quiet moment while she drank. She stilled, digesting. I watched myself watch her. "Mom?" I heard myself say. Then, as the vomit began, "Mommy?" The word was a surprise to me. I didn't remember saying it, and though anytime she called or texted, my phone glowed "Mommy," I couldn't remember the last time I'd spoken the word. I turned the volume down, watched vomit pour out of her, heard the noises I made, grunts like I was sick, too. I watched myself flit around the room, frantic, a bug in a jar, watched myself punch the call button on her bed. A voice came out of a speaker in the handrail.

"Can I help you?" It fuzzed, all static.

"An accident," I yelled.

Another wave of vomit, this one just bile. I ran to the bathroom, pulled clumps of paper towel from a dispenser, brought them back and covered my mother's chest. Her body waved again.

"Look at me," she wailed, and my face crumpled, ugly and small. There was another wave, then stillness. We waited. Finally, she began to move the paper over herself.

"I'll do it," I said, and she held up her hands to let me. But there weren't enough sheets. I was just pushing around the mess.

I stopped the video and pressed the button to delete.

13.

At the airport, I parked in the cell phone lot and disappeared into my phone, watching a weightlifter named Erin with 300,000 followers explain progressive overloading, watching a verified makeup artist explain her ten-step skincare routine. "If you do nothing else, SPF fifty," she said and waggled a tube at the screen. The story moved to a washed-up model's call to action, "Guys, the oceans are dying." She made namaste hands. I watched until the smell of vomit hit me, wafting off my sports bra like it had just splattered there. I looked around for nearby drivers, then peeled off the bra, careful with my arms, the sore spots on my breasts that kicked up when I lifted them. I chucked the bra to the floor and zipped into my hoodie. If I still smelled, it was just a faint whiff, a virtue signal, proof I was a good daughter, taking care.

"Here," my phone said. I propped it in the cupholder, joined the line of traffic snaking to arrivals. The gates were crowded. Everywhere people held up hands, phones, flagging. Leah stood among them, face in her screen. She seemed shorter than before, flanked on every side by men. I honked, waved, and she looked up, grabbed the handle of her suitcase and rolled toward me. Aside from a few awkward FaceTimes, it had been four years since I'd seen her. I was suddenly aware that those years were years in which we both had changed. It wasn't only me, becoming someone new. I watched her body expand as she neared the car, taller when she got close. She went to the back of the Prius and opened it.

"*Dooooomer*," I called from the front, putting on her old persona, my voice a silly snarl.

Her suitcase slid in and the back slammed. She walked around, landed in the passenger seat. "Hey," she said, affectless, as if she hadn't heard me. I felt myself inhale, sharp. She wasn't shorter, just wan like a consumptive, body folded in on itself, protective and weak.

"Hello?" she said, but I was staring at her kneecaps, popped up from the fabric of her leggings like baby skulls.

"Sorry," I said and cleared my throat. "Hi." We hugged. Muscle, bones, breasts. Against hers, my body felt animal and full. I pulled away first, reached for my phone. But cars honked behind me, every horn an echo. I put my hands on the wheel, signaled to turn, focused on the blinker's noise.

"I can't believe you made it," I said. "I couldn't believe it when you wrote back."

"Why?"

"I'm just happy you're here."

"Naurene is sick," she said, like she wasn't sure it was true, and wanted to confirm.

"And drugged. She's not herself. How are you?"

"What's that smell," she asked and I said, "Puke."

"Yours?"

"No."

We went quiet and I wondered how I'd survive her closeness, now that her body was so unlike what I'd expected.

"I'm on a running scholarship at uni," she said, breaking the silence. "It's a lot of pressure." Her voice was accented now, Australian, every R an A. I accelerated to fill a hole in the traffic's flow. The car beeped, urgent.

"It wants you to buckle your seatbelt," I said. She pulled the strap.

"I'd ask what you're up to," she said. "But I already know."

"What?"

She buckled, waved her phone at me.

"Oh," I said, "very funny."

"I know everything about you."

"Not everything."

She looked out the window. Strip malls spun by. When she spoke next, her words were slower.

"Fucking Texas," she said, reaching forward and turning her air vent so it blew toward me instead. Her sweatshirt was oversized but the sleeves were rolled up. I looked at her forearms, tan and furred, reminiscent of every health class PSA about eating disorders: anorexia, bulimia, laxative use, diet pills, compulsive exercise. As a girl she had been delicate, according to my mother, anyway. Then she had been buxom before it was time to be buxom, a little girl's soul, trapped in a bikini model's shape. Now she was just insufficient, her body like a winter coat designed for style, too thin to keep her warm.

Leah spoke about Australia for the rest of the drive. She used the word "pressure" a lot, said her parents worked obsessively, said she was lonely. She was acutely aware of her emotional landscape, her "problems," which surprised me.

"Running makes me sick," she said. "But I need it to get by. And to win, I need to stay small." She said that negotiating the cost of survival was the sad reality of global capitalism. That along with responding to humanitarian crises, rampant racism, cultural appropriation, and economic inequality, on a personal level we were all tasked with determining lesser evils. Which for her meant running and the dietary modifications she imposed upon herself to stay weightless and fast.

"People don't understand what it's like for me as a transplant," she said. "They think that just because Australians speak English it's not a totally different culture." She told me she was still a virgin. "Boys aren't interested," she said, and I wanted to help her. I considered suggesting she achieve a *curvier aesthetic*. Until recently, I hadn't realized that's what men wanted, so maybe Leah was the same, and simply didn't know. Then again, she had just told me she was small for a reason, sick for a reason. I didn't want to make her repeat it.

AT THE HOSPITAL I showed Leah the way to my mom like I hadn't just figured it out myself. She stood in the elevator, the doorway of my mom's room, with a shocked look on her face, a stuttering Skype. I walked in ahead, motioned at the blue chemo armchair.

"You sit there," I said loudly.

"Don't wake her," Leah said and sat. I went to the hallway for a smaller plastic chair, carried it back to the room in front of me like a battering ram. My mom's purse thunked against my hip; inside, pills rattled, my phone vibrated. I put the chair down across the bed from Leah, where I could see her, and checked my notifications: more responses to the pain-scale faces, the feminist reading list, the bruised and swollen lip injection selfie I'd reposted, trying to imply I was somewhere other than where I truly was, trying to imply a procedure that filled, rather than diminished. I shut the phone, put it on the seat, sat on its face.

Leah had balled up, arms wrapped around skulled knees. "Naurene looks old," she whispered and then, "I didn't mean that the way it sounds."

"It's okay," I said and we went quiet. My mother's body inflated, deflated, in the space between us. Her eyelids flitted open, shut.

"Mom," I said, loud enough to rouse her. "Look who's here."

"Naurene," Leah said.

My mom opened and closed her mouth.

"She's actually doing better," I said and wondered when I should tell Leah about the tumors. If I should tell her. As far as Leah was concerned, the surgery was exploratory, but so far inconclusive. I wasn't even sure my mother knew what the surgeon had found. And though I had intended to tell Leah in person, though I suspected it was my job to tell my mom as well, I was afraid to see either of them grieve. As if the pain of the women I loved might peel the lid off my own.

"Girls," my mom whispered and then, "Walk the dogs for me, will you?"

I turned to Leah. *Hallucinations*, I whispered knowingly. *The pain meds*.

"No dogs, Mom." I said, "Just us."

"Naurene, it is so good to see you," Leah said. Her face was unsticking, contorting into expressions I could no longer physically accomplish: a squinched frown, a lifted brow when she removed her glasses and wiped the tears away. I thought about how, as a child, she'd rarely cried. I had been the emotional one. And now? My mother reached her wired-up hand for Leah's hand, which uncoiled from inside the sleeve of her sweatshirt. I had a sudden urge to run, hide in a break room or linen cart. I picked up my phone.

"Get together for a picture," I said. Leah edged closer to the bed, holding tight to my mom's hand. "Closer." I waved. She hunched down beside the bed, tried to put her free arm around my mom, thought otherwise and placed an elbow on the mattress. I touched the shutter, looked to see the image: Leah, bone where the baby fat had been; my mom, pale and oddly childlike. Something about her mouth, the drugs, made her look like a kid with a retainer, lips puffed up over wire and bulk.

"No pain," she murmured.

"That's good," I said. Leah sat and I hid my phone. We asked questions, waited for answers my mother couldn't manage. I opened my phone again to read to the room, a news bulletin about special counsels and abuses of power, political stories I didn't follow but felt now that I should.

"Don't even get me started," Leah said.

My mother looked back and forth at each of us then closed her eyes. Normally, any mention of politics set her off, her voice picking up, fevered by certainty, causes she was certain were good and true and right. She was loud about what she believed in a way that made me want to temper her energy. My realism provided moderation. I had *realistic* assumptions about people and politics, men and power, women and what they'd do to stay close to men and power. My mother assumed all women were on her side, and she was shocked when this turned out to be untrue, as it often did. Mostly, she picked political fights with men, anyway. Doctors, post-office clerks, and dog-sitting clients; NA leaders, any man she could find, really. It was a test, to see if they'd admit their privilege and promise to do better. But it also appeared to be a sort of flirting, like she wanted to change their minds, not just about politics, but about her personal worth, which was also in question, though she wouldn't admit it. She focused on her chronic ailments instead. Excuses I had thought. And how wrong I'd been.

I finished reading the story and my voice trailed off, but I stayed inside my phone, the screen. From the corner of my vision, I saw Leah move to her bag, find her own phone, sit back down. When I looked up next, she was scrolling.

"TRY AGAIN TOMORROW, girls," Nancy the nurse said when she kicked us out. I wrote my number on the whiteboard, turned my ringer up. It was late, almost eleven, and Leah's flight was in the morning.

"I assumed they'd let us stay all night," she said.

I hadn't thought about how long we could visit, hadn't considered Leah had come for my mother only, and not at all for me. I drove us back toward the cottage. But I could tell she didn't want to see it.

"It's the same," I said, as if that wasn't what she feared.

"Can we stop at H-E-B?" she asked. "Grocery stores are the only American thing I miss."

"There's food at the house."

"Please," she said. "I came all this way."

We detoured to the twenty-four-hour branch on Montrose. Inside, we carried separate baskets in opposite directions. As soon as Leah disappeared, I fished my last hydrocodone from my mom's purse and swallowed, throwing my head back dramatically to get the pill to the back of my throat. It was something I'd seen Jake do. I took out my phone to check on him. He was another world, belonging to another world:

selfie-mode, tropical flowers tucked behind both ears. "Mood forever," hovered in modern font above his head.

"Baaaaabe," I commented, "don't forget about me," desperate.

The frame flipped. Jake laughed from behind the camera as two old men used pitchforks to drape a boa constrictor over a bro's meaty shoulders. In the background: a woman's playful scream.

I grabbed a bag of skinny chips off the shelf, threw it too hard into my basket, then replaced it with a fresh bag. In LA I ate what Jake ate only less of it, less often. Here, I could do what I wanted, binge if I wanted. Was that what I wanted? I wove up and down the aisles, phone out, watching stories, watching the light mirage as the pill metabolized. People pushed carts past mine. A man talked to his AirPods, "Well, the Pampers are on sale." Three kids petitioned their mom for cereal she said cost too much in sugar points. "Ninety grams!" she said, and the whines picked up. I turned the corner, made my way down the candy aisle. Every hungry shade of orange, yellow and red asked to be eaten. I stopped, considered the calories in a Reese's. I picked up a bar, checked the label, questioned my motives. *Are you really hungry?* read a Post-it stuck to my mother's fridge. The note had been there so long and had become so familiar that the question had gone invisible. But it was also constant, posed every time I opened my mouth to consume. No, I wasn't hungry, not for sugar, not then. But Leah's body, like my mother's, scared me. I wanted her to be healthy, alive. I wanted to shock her into nourishing herself. I had a feeling that if she didn't, I would have to, and caretaking Leah in addition to my mom was a burden I couldn't bear. For a moment, I imagined force-feeding her. *This is for your own good*, I would say, mashing meat into her mouth. But I didn't want to see her cry again.

As if I'd conjured her, Leah appeared at the other end of the aisle. She hesitated, then walked toward me. Her basket was still empty, and I thought that leaving it that way must mean she truly was sick, that starvation was a compulsion, not a choice the way she'd made it out to be. She'd asked to come here, to H-E-B, after all. But faced with all this bounty, she couldn't choose any of it. Only a moment before, I'd wanted to shame her into eating, to force her. But now, I saw that nothing I did would cure her. I put the Reese's back.

"I'm trying to find the yogurts," she said. Close up she looked overwhelmed, a little lost, but also prettier, her complexion warmed by the colors around us.

I held up my phone. "Will you help me?"

"You know where the yogurts are?" she asked.

"Yeah, after," I said, and she took the phone. "Get a lot," I said.

She sighed, dramatic, but let me show her how to position the screen. Then I put myself across the aisle from where she stood, so close to the Reese's, Snickers Bars, bags of M&M's, that I could smell their chocolate insides. I unzipped my hoodie to show my new cleavage and stood on my toes.

"This is stupid," Leah said, but I heard the shutter. I twisted, showed my ass and it clicked again.

"All set?" she asked.

"Come on," I said and faced her, pressed my torso toward the lens so my breasts were centered. I wet my lips, parted them. The shutter closed again, and again.

"Hello, excuse me, earth to the ladies?" An old woman with a cart wanted to get by.

"Sorry," we said and stepped aside. She grumbled as she passed and Leah said, "Sorry ma'am," then started to laugh. "Ma'am," she said again, her voice lighter, like she couldn't believe the word. Her laughter made mine kick up too. I moved to where she was, put my chin on her shoulder and touched the phone she held to scroll the shots.

"Dude, I know you got lips, but a boob job?" she whispered, still half laughing.

"I don't know, did I?" I whispered back.

"I don't know, did you?"

I tried to make my face a knowing smirk. "Who cares?" I said and then, "Cute." I tapped the screen to mark my favorites.

"Okay,' I said, "now you."

"No way."

"Do it," I whined, "just for fun." She slumped to where I had stood.

"Okay," I said, "face the candy then turn and look back over your shoulder." She made a purposefully ugly face. I pressed to catch her. Even a bad picture, tagged and shared to my account, could multiply her following by five, maybe ten. It wasn't the care she needed, it wasn't a cure. But it was something.

"Girl," I said, "your body is fire. Now turn back and put this leg forward—" I knew where to find her angles; they were my angles, too. "Yeah, like that and tip your hip, yeah, good." I shot her again. She smiled. For an instant, I saw my little girl friend and every character she had played. "Gorgeous," I said, and Leah's mouth parted, wanting, like mine. Abruptly, I lowered the phone.

"All done," I said and opened the images to see how she looked, angled right, directed. But in the pictures I'd taken, every bone protruded, every hollow held a shadow. I'd thought our angles were the same; I'd been wrong and didn't want to show her. But she came over to see and what choice did I have? I turned the screen and felt her change. She gave a little sigh. "Wow," she said, and I wondered if she'd cry.

"I look—I look kind of great." She took the phone from me without asking, pinched the screen. "AirDrop me?"

I TOOK SERVICE roads home, blinking extra to cut the painkillers' haze. We passed under I-10, a lit-up billboard Leah craned to see. *Pregnant? Scared?* next to a shadow of a crying woman, face in her hands. Leah said, "You know those crisis pregnancy centers are run by anti-abortionists, right? Like, under the guise of helping women."

I said, "Gross."

"They're considered offensive in Australia," she said, and I flared inside, like she thought they weren't offensive here, too. Like she thought her leaving, her political awakening, college education, had made her wise. "I used to only care about animals," she said. "But then I realized women are endangered too. The world is so fucked."

"Totally," I said, "the oceans are dying." I pulled in the driveway and sing-songed *here we are*, my voice high and chipper. Leah opened her door. The outside air had cooled.

"Maybe it'll storm and you'll get stuck," I said and wondered if that was what I wanted. Leah didn't answer. She let me carry her bag, followed me up the porch. I took a minute finding the right key, then pushed open the door, walked in ahead of her. She stopped on the threshold.

"It smells the same," she said. "Essence of you and Naurene."

"What do we smell like?"

"Bounce dryer sheets. I made my mom buy them for a while after we moved." She came all the way in, stood slumped in the kitchen like it defeated her to return.

"That's so cute," I said, searching my brain for similar proof of my love for her, the trauma of its loss. I thought so often of our childhood closeness. But after she left, I was the one who had ghosted, and now that we were together, closeness felt superficial and abstract, a viral aphorism, a meme.

"I have to pee," I said and left the bathroom door open, like we used to. As I listened to my piss hit the bowl, I wondered if what I missed was less Leah herself, than the time we shared before sharing time the way we did was either eroticized or patholo-gized; before it was consumed by men. I washed my hands then unzipped my sweatshirt even more, like she might take the hint and ask to see my implants. Suddenly, I wanted to show her, not sexually, but out of pride, like look at what I've acquired, look at how I've grown, look what can be achieved with positive thinking, high vibes. I came out and she went in, closed the door.

"I need a shower," she yelled from inside. I heard the lock.

I UNPACKED OUR food, refrigerated the cold stuff, peeled open the skinny chips I'd bought, created a stack. Chew-ing took a while and I felt the noise of each crunch, felt Leah would too. I clipped the bag, shelved it, ate two Xanax from the bottle I'd stashed in my mom's purse. I still had plenty. Dr. Holle had prescribed me a thirty-day supply. She'd refilled it when I called and followed a script Jake suggested.

"I thought the pills were something else and disposed of them," I'd said, my voice staged, unnatural. The nurses bought my story, or they didn't, but certainly they wouldn't buy it again.

I moved to the couch, checked other people's stories. Ella's, where she propped in a high-chair like a child and offered up the soft underside of her banded arm for a blood draw. A lab technician slapped the veins. The needle hit. Ella opened her mouth and her filtered lips jumped off the screen like a scream. "We're running tests for black mold biotoxins," she said. "At least I'm keeping my sense of humor." I watched through to Erin the fitness model, taking turns squatting in a Smith machine with her #workoutbestie, who had 20,000 followers, thick ankles and a fine but not #fine butt. First, Erin filmed her friend's ten reps, then the friend filmed Erin, pushing for twelve. The shot showed the branded ass of Erin's workout pants, ruched at the crack to make each cheek a separate entity. Swipe up for discount code. I swiped, but Leah's weight arrived on the couch beside me and I closed the sale page, turned the phone so she could see the girls.

"I thought you avoided strength training," she said. "Too much bulk."

"I mean, I thought that in high school," I said.

"So you lift now?"

"Sometimes," I lied.

She got up again, walked into the kitchen. I heard the fridge open and close. "When do you think you'll talk to Naurene's surgeon?" she called. I hesitated, watching her return. She held a sugar-free chocolate vanilla pudding cup. She'd purchased three packs from the store, saying she'd put the extras in her suitcase. The T-shirt she wore was nightgown sized, the outline of a running man and the words *Marathon* folded between her breasts, which seemed smaller now, like everything about her. She looked so fragile; I couldn't tell her. "Not sure," I said. "Tomorrow probably." She sat again, peeled the lid off her cup. I opened a highlight reel on Erin's account called *Booty Transformation!* and we watched in silence. Pictures of Erin, small like us, gave way to pictures of goals she had set and realized on the way to her present 🍑. It felt good to see her grow, a sign of life, a positive example, the power of persistence. I thought of Jake, the pulls-ups he did from a bar in his closet, how he could lift his own weight like it was nothing, how when I tried, I couldn't leave the ground, and both of us had laughed about it.

When the highlights ended, Leah leaned over me and touched the screen to see Erin's entire grid.

"I think she got a butt lift," she said.

"I want a pudding," I said and went to the kitchen. I had wanted her to ask me about my implants, but now I wanted to avoid them. I wanted to be strong on my own, like the weight-lifter girls, so different from what Leah had become.

"Get me another," she called from the couch and I carried two cups back, passed her one. She put my phone down to take it and I watched her dip the small spoon she'd picked from the drawer of big ones into the shiny chocolate surface. She lifted a sliver to her mouth and held it there.

"Remember high school Marcus?" she asked, speaking around the metal. "You still talk to him?"

"Not really, not lately." I opened my cup. "He's whatever." I wanted to tell her about Jake but was afraid of what she'd say.

"What about you?" I asked. "Boys? Girls? Anyone you like?"

"No," she said. "I already told you I never really made friends in Australia."

"Sounds hard," I said and went quiet, trying out excuses for why I'd ghosted her: when you left it felt like I'd done some-thing to deserve it; since then my only friends have been guys and they don't know me like you do; for months after you moved I rode my bike by your house until a new family moved in and I stopped; I have a selfish personality; abandonment issues.

"At uni—" she started, but my phone buzzed with meaningless notifications. I let them drown her out.

"Selfie," I said, and turned the screen to face us.

"I look gross," she said.

"I can Facetune." I wedged myself close. She smiled without teeth. I made a fish face. Next shot she tried on my expression and I kissed her cheek, then flipped the phone and got lost favoriting what I'd edit later.

"I'm tired," she finally said. "Should I sleep in your room?"

"My mom's bed is the big one," I said, still scrolling. "We can both stretch out."

She got up, took her half-eaten pudding back to the kitchen. The fridge opened and shut.

"I'd rather sleep alone," she said.

I put the phone down, watched her walk into my room. I went to the door, considered how to protest, but she was already sitting on the mattress, setting an alarm.

"Sweet dreams," she said without looking up.

"You too," I mumbled and returned to the couch, my phone, scrolling, waiting, as if she might talk to me from the other side of the wall between us. When we were girls she went through a phase where she muttered in her sleep, hidden messages I listened for and reported in the morning. "What does it mean?" I asked. Only sometimes did she know.

I DIDN'T THINK I'd sleep but woke and knew I had. Outside, in the live oaks, the grackles croaked. I opened Instagram, searched Jake and found nothing new. I got up, checked my bed, tossed and empty. I checked the kitchen, the bath, my mother's room. Leah's bags were by the front door. But she herself was gone. "Where you at?" I texted then made a pot of coffee. I dumped extra Splenda in my cup and took it to the porch to sit and wait and edit the H-E-B images. I opened my photos folder, scrolled past the pictures I'd shot of Leah, to my own unfiltered reflection. Cast in the harsh grocery store light, I looked exhausted and overcooked, like I'd spent the day tanning, stocking up sweat and skin damage. I flipped to the next shot, the big reveal. My tits looked too high to be real, too firm to be a pleasant simulation of realness. I swiped back to Leah, bare faced and bony, her eyelashes colorless wisps. "Wow," she had said. "I look kind of great." Maybe she was right; maybe she did. Maybe I was the sick one, unable to tolerate the prospect of her beauty, that she might share it and be loved. I put down the phone, stared hard through the wet scrim of spring air until I saw her on the other side—a speck, a shadow, a girl—and the scrim lifted.

"I just had to run," she said, and climbed the steps.

"There's coffee," I said. "What do you eat for breakfast?" She pulled her phone from a zippered pocket in her leggings, checked the time.

"We should go," she said.

In the car she read her emails. Too early for traffic, we sailed I-45 toward Galveston, where the highway ends. When we were freshly teenaged, even before learner's permits and licenses, my mother had moved to the passenger seat and let us take turns driving the last strip of road, to where the ocean begins.

"We could keep going," I offered. Leah typed, said nothing. "Remember our spot on the beach?"

Her fingers stopped but she didn't look up. "Of course I do," she said.

AT THE TERMINAL, we stood on the curb and hugged. The hug lasted, or it didn't, but I closed my eyes long enough to see images: the egg white bites and skinny latte I would order from Starbucks on the way to the hospital; the blurry mother who waited there; Jake's red-lit bedroom. All of it arranged, unfiltered, on a private grid.

"You could stay," I said as Leah pulled off.

"I know she will get better," she said.

"Don't go," I said and wondered if I meant it. "Don't forget me."

Her face had locked up again and the sky still looked like a storm. "I'm not going to forget you," she said, and I could tell it annoyed her to have to say it.

"I love you Leah," I said but she was already walking, already too far gone. A revolving door enveloped her body, spit it out behind a long window. She looked for signs, found a line and joined it. From the center console, my phone buzzed and Jake's name, a picture of his pewter contacts and prayer beads, wrote itself across the screen.

PART THREE

14.

Nighttime now. I stumble from a Lyft into the lobby of the Princess Hotel. It's been thirty-three hours since I left for the Aesthetica Center, most of which I've spent unconscious, sleeping in a recovery suite, my body working to stave off infection. I should do more to thank this body, I think, and pull the cords of my sweatshirt's hood, tightening the cocoon around my head. Beneath it, I'm fully masked by layers of gauze, a sterile sheet of ice Velcroed to my face. My face, beaten like a prize fighter's, my head, toggled by twin tubes hooked to clear containers the shape and size of lemons, filling with my watery blood.

I knew, going in, to expect incisions and drains, knew to expect I might not wake. "Not my first rodeo," I said when Dr. Perrault asked if I'd had anything to eat or drink since midnight, asked if I'd taken any pills. I lied and he reiterated the risks, the healing process, the first twenty-four hours of which I would be most susceptible to infection. "Expect to be shocked," he said, which was what I wanted. I wanted drastic transformation, wanted to watch myself come back slowly in the bathroom mirror, reborn from blood and bruises, all that violence. The in-between time, before results are final, is my favorite of any procedure, a time when I can be sick, but not truly, just stationed in bed, popping painkillers, my body working to heal, my brain acclimating to the bruises and swelling until one day they're gone and the transformation is complete. I'm old enough to know that this is how true transformation works, in increments so small you don't notice until one day you wake up and realize you've changed.

I touch the bundle around my head, stumble fast toward the elevator. The last dregs of anesthesia in my blood make me feel like I'm sleepwalking, which is not unpleasant. Even when I arrive at the elevator bank and find a family of tourists waiting—a mom and dad and their two boys—I'm okay with it.

"Good evening," I say, a phrase that leaves my mouth in an awkward clump, each word too formal. "Evening," says the father. He nods curtly, then wraps an arm around his wife. The children shuffle backward, hide behind their mother's shorts, and I realize they all bear horrified expressions.

"Go ahead," I mutter when the elevator arrives. "I'll get the next one."

"You sure?" the dad says, turning back once his kids are safe inside. I make a waving motion like *please*, and the doors close without me.

I zone out waiting for the next ride. Seconds pass but it all feels longer. Then the doors open and I usher myself through them. Inside, my indistinct reflection in the metal walls makes me think of Dr. Perrault, the hand mirror he held for me when I woke up.

"This'll be a bit scary," he said, and I brushed him away. I didn't want to see. Now, in the wavy distortion of the elevator, I'm still hidden, which makes me feel hopeful, on the way to something, some new stage of life where I'll find myself, wise and appropriate, a woman, a mother, and no longer a girl.

HE WAS MY age, Dr. Perrault, with a round face and neatly trimmed beard, a head of thinning hair. When we met in pre-op, I stared too long probably, trying to determine how there isn't a better treatment for baldness. So much science can solve about women's bodies—boobs, butts, labia, anything that sags. But how to fix a thin dick, a receding hairline, remains a mystery. Which feels fair, actually. Men can lean on other things. I once watched a *60 Minutes* segment on incels, the online communities they've fostered, the "looksmaxxing" (healthy eating, working out) they suggest to land "Stacys" (women), the limitations of "hard looksmaxxing" (plastic surgery) for men, and the "moneymaxxing" they suggest as alternate routes to Chaddom. Even the incels know they don't need beauty to ascend.

Career, money, a blue and black Ferrari, according to Instagram, Dr. Perrault has all that, which for a man, is better than a snatched jawline or a full head of hair. He scanned my face with his patented Aesthetica™ 4D wand, the size and shape of an ancient car phone, a screen on the top. It beeped as he passed it across my skin. Then he gave me two Valiums and drew a purple pen over my cheekbones, jaw, chin, and nose with short, staccato strokes. He stood back to survey his work, comparing the lines he'd made to what he read on the screen of his wand. I watched his eyes dart over my face.

"Gorgeous," he said and stared for a moment longer, awkward like a child, totally confident I wouldn't care, which I didn't. I liked the attention, felt validated in the surgeon's line of sight, an object to be fixed. He saw what I saw, the asymmetry, the age, everything I've done to try and hide it. And this made me love him.

He moved to the counter, unscrewed a tub of numbing cream, scooped out a handful and slathered my face. The gel was cold and reminded me of ultrasounds, babies, fresh infant skin.

"Alright Anna," he said and returned to his computer, clicked around. A three-foot screen hung on the wall next to my seat and suddenly it illuminated. A photograph presented itself, bright and giant. A face. Not my face, not quite. "So, looking at the image you provided for context," Dr. Perrault said, "we see a normal progression of aging for a woman in her middle thirties who has not undergone cosmetic enhancements of any kind. Some jowling here—" he pointed at the face's lower half. "Some recession here," he pointed at the chin. "But overall, a nice, natural template for your procedure. Tell me, did your mother seem to have early onset hereditary neck laxity?"

"I honestly don't recall," I said, staring at her picture. "I was only six when this photo was taken."

It was an image snapped in someone's backyard. Flowers and a fence I didn't recognize set the scene behind her. I'd dug it up from a physical album full of analogue relics, then scanned and cropped it to zoom in on my mother's face, fine lines around her mouth suggesting that she often smiled, forehead elevens suggesting that she frowned, furrows beneath her eyes where tears sometimes settled.

Dr. Perrault clicked some buttons and the image changed. It was the Aesthetica™ scan he'd just performed, an interactive map of my face. Colors differentiated what was real from what was fake. Red stood for musculature, white for filler, gray for implants, blue for scar tissue.

"Alrighty," the doctor said and handed me a mirror. I lifted the glass, winced, lowered it.

"If I may," he said and touched my arm to return the mirror to eye level. He pointed at the marks he'd made. "Our goal will be to remove all signs of previous enhancements, including the extensive filler fatigue we see on your face presently. I'll be dissolving all of that crap on the operating table to begin. Next, we'll make a series of incisions along the lateral hairline to remove the cheek implants you had placed, then work our way down to the jaw implants here." He motioned with a swirling gesture at my jaw. "We'll excise the calcified biostimulatory filler which, as you know, cannot be dissolved, and remove the surrounding scar tissue in the chin area. We'll also address the multiple past rhinoplasties by widening and aging your nose with cadaveric cartilage grafts." He cleared his throat. "Excuse me. We'll then remove the dermis—"

"What's that?" I asked.

"The top layer of skin," he said and I felt thrilled, slightly nauseous. "We'll remove the dermis and, using my custom Aesthetica™ technique, we'll stretch and replace it. For a final touch, we'll use my UV resurfacing laser to simulate some of the natural signs of aging such as sun damage, fine lines and wrinkles we see here on your mother. Sound good?"

"Yes," I said and thought my voice sounded confident and sure. He placed a hand on my shoulder. Yes, I was sure.

"Alrighty, let that numbing cream soak in a bit more." He left the room. Alone, I lay there, wondering if I felt the Valium, wondering if I could ask for more. I have a benzo tolerance built up but didn't want to tell Dr. Perrault about it. As if he might call off the procedure over a minor addiction, as if he might think me special, for needing what so many people need to stay alive.

I closed my eyes, listened to the pop music blossoming from the speaker, frantic. Music is so canned now, so obviously built to brainwash, I remember thinking that, remember trying to feel the drugs, count breaths.

There was a knock at the door, which opened before I said yes, enter, hello.

"It's Nurse Esther," said a nurse I hadn't met yet. "How we doing?"

"Good," I tried, my face too numb to talk.

"Looks good," she said, leaning in to see the drawings on my face. Her body reminded me of a cake pop, round on top, thin at the bottom, but ultimately short. Height, a particularly tricky physical trait to solve. The only surgery adds only an inch and costs a fortune, not worth the sacrifice for most. I should count myself lucky, I thought, for having the freedom to change myself this way. I should focus on living my lucky life, enjoying my privilege, rather than fixating on the problems I've created. But it was too late to back out. Esther was holding the mirror for me, showing me my marked-up face again, the lines on my skin like wrinkles, but also like a language I couldn't read, a surgeon's secret code. I felt excluded by the conversation he would have with my face, just the two of them under the lights in the operating theater, and passed the mirror back. In the process, my hand accidentally brushed Esther's breast. Neither of us acknowledged the contact. She pulled a phone from her pocket, checked the time.

"Ready to go back?" she asked. I nodded, yes. Ready. She helped me out of the chair, walked me down the hall, past the obnoxious pop art hung on every door, canvases featuring old cereal box characters painted into selfie poses: the Trix Rabbit making a kiss face, Cap'n Crunch giving peace fingers, Snap, Crackle and Pop throwing what looked like gang signs. I realized then how high I was. High and thinking about Leah, girlhood, Rice Krispies breakfasts, how we'd put our ears to our bowls, receive messages before we ate, as if each kernel of dehydrated rice had a body, a soul. Little Leah would narrate

Snap, Crackle and Pop's pleas for mercy in an array of squeaky voices—*please don't eat me.* Little Leah would have loved this heinous art.

Esther patted the metal table. "Hop right up," she said. I eased aboard, shivered. Everything surgical is always cold. "You want a blanket?" she asked. I thought I'd say no but told her yes. She laid it over me and it was pure pleasure, a bath towel from the dryer on a winter night.

"Thank you," I said.

"You're welcome, honey," she said and I drifted a little, into the painting hung high on the wall, Tony the Tiger in a track-suit, swinging an arm like he was saying *they're grrrrreat*, like you were supposed to wake up, see him there, and know you were great, also; you were gorgeous, alive; you went under, got that close to death, and made it back.

From the corner of my eye, I saw Dr. Perrault enter through an open door, gloved hands held up, brown with Betadine, sterile and safe. Esther put a shower cap on. She said, "Okay, let's count, honey," and lowered a mask over my mouth. "Count, honey," she said, "count." Her voice was an open door. I walked through it.

15.

I watched Leah leave, I answered Jake's call, lurching through airport traffic to the fracture of his Bluetoothed voice saying, "Babe, babe, baby," until the connection shored up and I said, "I miss you." It was true, and though honesty had felt needy before, now it felt warranted; I didn't want Jake to underestimate my love and leave me, too.

"How's your mom?" he asked and then, before I answered, he said, "Listen, big news, Blaze Cannabis needs someone last minute. A promotional party in Arizona. I threw out your name and they want you."

"Fuck," I said.

He said, "One night, you stand around, look hot and smoke weed. I got them up to seven K. They'll send a plane tomorrow." I merged onto a mottled access road. Out the window, a jackhammer punched potholes into dust.

"Fuck," I said again. "I don't know if I can, call you back?"

There was silence and I thought the call had dropped. I touched the screen. Jake was still there and spoke again in a burst of words, his voice high pitched, unfamiliar.

"Yeah, I mean, totally, if you can't you can't, but it would be a big favor to me, I mean, after your surgery and the flight to Houston and all—" He was still talking, and the jackhammer was still stuttering, when, as if in spasm, my hand reached out, and touched the red circle to hang up. I sat there for a moment, staring at what I'd done. Someone honked behind me and I drove forward, eyes on the road, then on the phone again, waiting for Jake to call back. But when he did, I couldn't make myself answer. This was the job I'd been waiting for; Blaze, the money, was everything I wanted. So why was I afraid to take it?

AT THE HOSPITAL my mother slept, unchanged. Nurse Nancy was gone, "Grace" written on the whiteboard in her place. I balled up in the recliner like Leah had, my phone warm as a hand in my hand, buzzing when Jake called back, when he texted, "No service?" and, "Call me." I ignored the notifications. A strange feeling, watching him want me and wanting him too, but also fearing what he offered.

Grace came in and out of the room. She lifted my mom's gown to check the bandages around her waist, then moved to the IV, unscrewed caps she wiped with alcohol and plugged into my mother's arm.

"This is Zofran for the vomiting," she said. "She'll be better now."

"Who is?" My mother was waking up.

"You'll be," Grace said.

"Oh," my mom said, "sorry."

"Honey, you're fine." Grace said it like she'd already had to more than once. My mother's apologies were punctuation and had been for as long as my memory. Even as she scrubbed period blood, read feminist fairy tales, the word *sorry* was a tick. It was, I remembered then, what she said when Leah moved away.

"Not your fault," she had said, and held me as I cried. "I'm sorry honey, I'm sorry, I'm sorry."

"Where's Leah?" she asked me now, as Grace fussed with wires.

"She left," I said.

My mom said, "Itchy, I think maybe bugs?" She looked from me to Grace.

"Bugs where?" Grace asked and my mom was quiet, thinking.

"No honey," Grace said, and something about Dilaudid. I opened my phone, the screen where I was *astonishing, sweet, sexy, stelle*, not a botched best friend, not a child, helpless while my mother pleaded—*I'm sorry, don't leave, don't yell, I'm sorry but you don't understand this world of hurt.* On Instagram I was @annawrey, neither myself, nor someone else, a fantasy worth 60,000 followers. As a Blazed Bud I could be loved beyond 100,000; as a Blazed Bud, I could be worth as much as Erin the weightlifter, Ella, my father, that forgotten time before Leah, where memory began. And after that, I'd never be alone again. I imagined myself, lit up in green, posted to @BlazeCannabis. I imagined the flurry of likes and follows and jobs that would come next, how a whole week would be swallowed by the excitement of their attention, their commitment to the dream I sold, the envy and want @annawrey triggered every time I posted.

"Bugs in the bed," my mother was saying, "I feel them in the bed."

I got up, pretended to make a call, then stood outside, counting breaths and listening to Grace bargain.

"Honey," she said, "the itch means you're healing—doctor says you'll be going home soon."

Soon my mother would be home. Soon she would be in recovery and need me there, need the $7,000 I could earn in one night away from her. If I went, I would be back within a day; she would never have to know. And I would give her every penny, a good daughter, a daughter who seized the opportunity to provide, and to caretake. It was an opportunity I'd lose forever if I didn't hurry up. The phone was in my hand, the call I hadn't placed was a door inside the screen. I entered numbers to unlock it, and pressed Jake's name.

16.

I get to the Princess Suite, fish the keycard from my hoodie pocket, swipe to unlock the enormous, weighted door. The room has been serviced since I left, hours and days and lifetimes ago, and smells less fungal. Either that or my senses are dulled. I beeline for the bathrobe, folded now on the corner of the bed, and slip myself inside its safe embrace. I ease under the covers and turn on the TV. A model with deep black skin and a shaved head stomps around a shiny, wet, fake New York. *Your loss, Bro*, a knowing voiceover commands. I stare. I like this woman's story, would like to buy the mascara she's selling and support her efforts to show Bro what he's lost. The commercial floats into a tampon ad and I listen to another woman's voice, telling me what I need to be happy like her.

I WAKE UP an hour later and the TV's still flashing. I have to pee. This is a positive sign, a sign the anesthesia is almost all worn off, which I'm supposed to want. Every hour that passes between this new face, new life, and the surgery I lived through to get them, shows me I can survive; I can be different from

Naurene, @annawrey. But first, I have to get to the toilet. I have to pass the mirror and face myself, which I've successfully avoided until now. I cross my legs, squeeze, wait until I can wait no longer.

The bathroom light, that now-familiar hum, makes me black out for a moment when I flip the switch. I hold the doorframe, wait for my eyes to adjust, then shuffle in, bunch up the robe, sit. Painkillers make my pee slow. But I wait, patient, and like an old friend, it returns, falls to the bowl. I sit there a while after it's over. Gingerly, I stand, flush, turn to see myself.

It's like seeing a mean email, a troll's nasty DM, Jake. It's like seeing every mistake I've ever made, blown up and blistered on my own skin, almost beautiful in its honesty. I was supposed to be prepared for this. *Following surgery, it's important you don't make any major decisions, operate any heavy machinery or rush to self-judgement during the first seventy-two hours*, said the paperwork I signed at the Aesthetica Center. *Not my first Rodeo*, I said, so I should know the drill now, know how to recover. Still, I'm shook. More than that, I'm hot, flushed with fever. I touch my forehead: clammy, not burning. I'm not infected, not literally. I'm finally fixed. Finally, I'm 😍, 💜, *astonishing*, 🔥, *sweet*, 💞, *sexy, stelle*, 👍, 👌, 😍💕💯🖤❤️💜❤️. And I'm full of rage. I touch my phone, open Instagram, navigate once more to my @annawrey inbox, the *Vanity Fair* reporter's string of DMs—*you could make a real difference to other women*—then to my finsta, then to Jake's account. *Staycation!* his story still chortles. *It's so important to spend quality time with family*, he tells his followers, in the service of the resort that sponsors his posts. I take my keycard, run my finger over its sharp sides, move my eyes around the room and look for other edges. There it is, the steak knife, still waiting at my bedside. I go to it, take it by the hilt. Wood and steel, serration and a single point. They fit into my hand. The door to the Princess Suite bangs behind me as I leave.

17.

"You literally need nothing," Jake said. Makeup, clothing, food and drink, all provided. I went home and packed. My toothbrush, my phone, my wallet and pills. They rattled in my backpack as I climbed the gangplank of a private plane en route from New York, stopped in Houston just for me. It was bright out, early morning, that kind of light. It changed when I stepped inside, turned to holes, then girls. Glossed and fresh. Girls like that, I'd thought they weren't real; when I saw them on Instagram I'd thought they were filtered, Photoshopped. But I'd been wrong. I stood in the door, scanned for a seat, counted. Six espresso-brown blow outs, six boob jobs, six Botoxed foreheads. Six bodies, made like mine, only better, more beautiful, beautiful like I knew I'd never be.

"Hi," I said. A few girls looked up from their phones, responded with muffled *Heys*. I slunk to an empty seat and the plane became a guttural whine beneath us. We rolled down the runway. The roll turned to a surge, and speed. I tried to relax my face. We lifted into the air and the whine got louder.

Girls adjusted sleep masks, headphones; they reclined their chairs, shifted, settled. I balled up and watched the world shrink.

From a distance, Houston looked ugly as ever, skyscrapers zoned next to churches next to cul-de-sacs; roads at interrupted angles, all cracked. Whoever thought it was a good idea to build helter-skelter on a wetland? Nature always pushed up from underneath. Pythons and gators in the bayou, sewage in the street when it rained too hard. But the sunsets, thick and pink. The bats that roost in colonies under bridges, patterns over the dusk when they hunt.

We jutted through a cloud layer and all that disappeared. I took a Xanax from the bottle in my bag. The pilot came over the intercom, called the cabin *ladies*, announced our altitude. I dozed off, woke to his voice. "Truth or Consequences, New Mexico," he fuzzed, "named, believe it or not, after a radio quiz show popular in the 1950s." The girl next to me rolled her eyes and opened a pack of gum. I tapped her shoulder and she lifted her headphones.

"Could I?" I pointed to the gum and she held out the pack.

"This your first time with Blaze?" she asked.

"Yeah," I said.

"Sedona is a spiritual place," she said and put her headphones back on.

I had heard it before. A month before I left for LA, my mother had made an appointment with a new naturopath. "The ache," she'd said, "it's deeper lately," and asked me to drive her.

The office was on the seedy side of South Houston, manned by a woman with chin hair, a binder of prescriptive herbs. "You harbor hatred," she told my mom. "It's a toxic place to come from." She suggested tinctures, meditation, a retreat she hosted in a Sedona vortex. Three thousand for the weekend. "Toxicity blocks a body," she warned. "Tumors, artery clogs. You need to cleanse."

"Three thousand isn't feasible," my mother said, her voice at its most Southern. I thought that meant she had the woman's number. But she paid a hundred dollars for an ionic footbath session, my mom with her feet in a magnetized tub of water that frothed blue and gray the longer she sat. The gray was heavy metal, the naturopath said, the blue was intestinal sludge.

"I feel cleared out," my mom said after. We left with the pain shrunk and managed, but three days later it returned like it had rested and grown.

"That bitch," I said and googled footbath science, discovered the scam.

"Absolutely N-O," my mom said, from the couch. "Women don't call other women the B-word."

"Starting our descent," the pilot told the plane. I felt my guts move to one side, then lurch to the other. Girls adjusted their chairs. "Seatbelts," the pilot said. I felt full, bloated. Something I ate, something I wanted and didn't eat. I squeezed myself, imagined explosion. Small planes, prone to nosedives. Bodies, prone to betrayal. I shouldn't have come. I should have stayed with my mother. The wheels came out with a troubled clunk.

I was sweating. We sped up, touched down. The pilot hit the brakes, hard at first, then easier.

We rolled around the tarmac, stopped where a white Escalade was parked, every door open. I hustled for the jet's bathroom, soft-lit with fancy soap and a built-in compartment filled with Magnum condoms, gold foil packets like complimentary sweets. I kneeled at the metal mixing bowl toilet. Footsteps from below made the floor shake. The plane lightened with every bag taken from its insides. I had to hurry, but the vomit I'd been sure was imminent wasn't coming. I wanted it now and retched to cleanse. Only dry air came out. I made my fingers the shape of a gun, stuck them down my throat, deep where the bones were.

I had never been an effective purger. "A sensitive gag reflex," Jake said once, and suggested I practice with a banana. Maybe he was right—his cock made me gag. But my hand never could. I removed it, wiped my palm on my pants. "Jesus," I said to no one, and shut the lid.

I was last down the gang plank. Arid and altitude met me. And a man in wrap-around sunglasses who motioned me into the car. Inside, the other girls were buckled up, taking selfies, everyone awake now. The door slammed behind me. "You okay, hon?" someone asked. "Airsick," I said, expecting sympathetic words, murmurs, something. But the car was quiet after. Out of the airfield, onto a two-lane road, through town, girls held phones to windowpanes, filming despite the tint: signs for aura photographs and crystals and chakra balancing. I lifted my phone to join them but felt sick again and pressed the screen between my palms instead.

We climbed a hill, descended. The landscape changed to desert, broken fences, broken storefronts, the words "Indian Jewelry" "frybread" and "pottery," painted on every wall. The girls kept filming and I thought about Leah, what she'd said about America, privilege, appropriation, words I knew but couldn't use. I was guilty of all of it, that much I understood. As were the girls around me, witlessly consuming real need, real people's stories, to upload later as sidebars to their own. I put my head on the window, forehead against cold glass, and listened to their chatter. This filter, that filter, my mom this and that. *Say Yes to the Dress*. HIIT versus bootcamp versus cardio versus weights. CBD versus THC. Botox versus Dysport. Adderall versus caffeine, coke versus molly. Vodka diet, vodka sugar-free Red Bull, tequila soda, extra lime.

"Hold your pulse points," someone told me.

"Thanks," I said, and dug a thumb into my wrist.

We slowed to turn. Another road, this one private. It took us to a gate, tall as a house. The driver rolled down his window, spoke to the man in white who guarded it. The gate opened and we passed into a compound, peppered with small buildings, golf carts and four-wheelers. We turned a corner, approached a mansion so large it looked like a shopping mall. Through the window tint, I saw Jake descend the front steps.

He hadn't said he would be here. I hadn't asked where he would be. It struck me as strange, that I hadn't thought to ask.

Because seeing him felt like wanting and working and coming so close to having. It felt like elation and dread. The car stopped. Doors opened. Girls rushed out. Jake orchestrated bags. I came last, put myself in his way.

"What are you doing here?" I asked. He jerked a little, like he hadn't expected to see me.

"There you are," he said, and took hold of my shoulders, pulled me in, hugged me, pushed me out again and looked at my breasts.

"I'm so happy to see you," he said.

"I'm feeling sick." I stuck out my tongue.

"I'll get you something for that." He kissed my forehead. I asked again why he was around, but it was simple, Jake said. He owed Blaze a favor. He sometimes helped Blaze out. Remember that time he came to Arizona? He came to Arizona a lot. He didn't have to explain beyond that, or tell me to follow. I just followed; all the girls followed. Up the stairs, into the house, through the wide foyer and grand lobby, past red lights and houseplants big as trees, an elevated scaffolding and turntable. Speakers pumped trap music, stopped for a sound check, started again. Men stood around in black athleisure and white sneakers. And everywhere, the Blaze brand insignia, that neon-green panther, bore its fangs.

Jake led us to the middle of the room, then turned around to face us like a tour guide. "Some of you know the drill," he said. "Bags open, IDs out." Two men went purse to purse, checked IDs, offered iPads, electronic forms cued up on the screens. "For insurance," Jake said. "Everyone has to sign."

We all signed. There was some laughter over the difficulty of doing anything with acrylic tips. A few of the girls already had them, prosthetic talons shaped like coffins. Upstairs we'd each receive fresh sets, neon green with panther stickers. We would cohere, down to the nails.

We wanted to cohere. The infinity pool and movie theater and bowling alley, we wanted to see them. We wanted our manicure, blow out, wax, spray tan.

We walked in a group fronted by Jake. Through the house, into an elevator, everyone excited. *Musical guest*, we chattered, *product, champagne, Blaze*. Jake stood close, took my hand, squeezed it. "Open up," he said and fed me a pill. I swallowed, smiled my trademark smile.

"How's your mom?" he asked.

"Okay," I said. "Better."

The doors opened. Jake showed us to a room as big as a small club, with makeup chairs and plastic tents for tans and modesty curtains that hid wax tables, massage tables. And everywhere girls, seated and splayed, phones up, selfie-ing, a surround-sound Beyonce sing-along.

"Ella will help you out," Jake yelled to our group over the din. "Ella!" he yelled even louder. She arrived wearing a white tracksuit, holding a rose gold iPad.

"Overseeing the flow of traffic," she said. I elbowed past a few girls to get close to Jake.

"Now I feel out of the loop," I said. I hadn't expected Ella, just as I hadn't expected Jake. But Ella's presence was a relief.

Maybe we would spend the whole party together; having her around to show me the ropes was preferable to being alone.

Jake kissed my cheek. "Ella knows what you need," he said.

I said, "You okay?"

He kissed me on the mouth, called me baby. "Just have fun," he said, and was gone again.

THE GET-READY ROOM was like a triage unit, everyone there to cure or be cured. In the back there was a table with food on it, orange juice, champagne. I walked over, ate a peach, watched Ella put girls in chairs and note what services they needed. I finished the fruit in three bites and my brain fizzed. I mashed another into my mouth and my body began to settle, with pills or food, I didn't care. I was okay, it would be okay, only my first time, no way I was supposed to know what to expect. I was chewing when Ella came to me.

"I'm so tired," she said and air-kissed my cheeks.

"What about that biotoxin test?" I asked. "Any answers?"

She looked at her iPad.

"My mom—" I started, like Ella should know about the option of elective surgery, the imperative to push for answers.

"You need everything, yeah?" she interrupted.

"Yeah," I said, "everything." She pointed to a chair, eyes still on the iPad. I went to it, feeling in the way, a fangirl not a star. Ella had shared her health problems with the world, asking for help. But now that I'd mentioned them, now that I'd tried to help and failed, I felt like a creeper for having noticed. I sat, hung my backpack on the armrest, took out my phone and filmed myself, kitten filtered, while a girl gave me a blowout; 'sexy baby' filtered, while a girl gave me a manicure. I shared, tucked the phone under my butt. I could feel it there, buzzing with 😊😅😂😸 as a sullen girl gave me mink lashes that brushed my lids when I blinked. I moved next to a table where another girl plucked hair from my bikini line, armpits, ass, with little strips of wax, to keep the red down. I followed a girl to a plastic tent, left my phone outside. Inside, I got naked and she stuck panther-headed pasties to my nipples. I wanted her to mention my breasts, but when she didn't, it felt womanly, and I wondered if it was in her job description never to comment on clients' bodies.

She started up a spray gun and hosed me with brown tanner that sloshed in its chamber as she moved around, instructing me into poses that helped her cover every spot. The liquid made me think of my mom, the Diet Coke bile she vomited, the same color as my body, drenched now in paint. It washed off an hour later, though, left me the right kind of orange, pale only where the pasties had hidden me, same as the other girls. Taped into our Blaze uniforms, we were almost identical, different only slightly in tan tone, hair color, height. We were a type, and took selfies to show the world the similarity of our bodies, smushed together to fit the same size screen, broken apart while we scrolled, assessing the images we made, then posted to endless, endless 😺😿💚🤍🖤💚💚💚💚🤍🖤💚💚💚 💚💚🤍🖤💚🖤.

AT DUSK, WE left our phones in the room and posed by the pool with CBD cocktails, a formation of fifty. The photographer was @Chrisss, Ella's boyfriend. "Smile, ladies," he called. Now candid. Now jump. We screamed for the camera, leaped for it. The flash snapped, our drinks spilled, my breasts felt leaden and sore. We landed. Beyond us, water touched sky and sun, slipping.

After, Ella moved us back to the get-ready room, which had been freshened. Tables with champagne and vodka, coke on a plate, doll-size spoons around it in a fan. We all rushed first to our phones. I went next to the drug, but Ella called me back to a line she'd assembled. "Hair and makeup check," she said and bodies milled around, fixing. Fingers grazed my face, gentle with my skin the way I never was. The silk feathers of a contouring brush felt like my mom's touch, how she'd pet my cheeks to wake me when I fell asleep on the couch watching *Housewives*, or in the car on the ride home from Galveston, the beach, endless afternoons in the water with Leah. "Honey, put your shoes on," she would say, "we're home."

The door opened and brought new music, men's voices. It closed behind Jake, @Chrisss, a white-sneakered entourage, and Blaze, who yelled, "Heyo, hot girls." His voice was high, squeaky. He was short, but walked the line of us like a shadow, stretched tall by changing light. He had a bag of powder on him and offered it to some girls he passed. I thought of nightmares, how if this were one of mine, Blaze would stop at me, and I would know to fear him, I would know to scream.

I counted girls, three before he reached me, then two, then one. Sweat stung my pits where the wax had ripped. I felt my heart pick up. Blaze stopped where I waited. He held up the baggie and spoon. My fingers shook when I touched his hand to lift the spoon closer. He flinched. I hesitated. He moved the spoon, the hand that held it, down to his crotch.

"On your knees," he said and looked over his shoulder at the men. I froze, glanced at Jake, whose face was blank.

"Just kidding," Blaze said and lifted the spoon. I smiled, in on the joke. Inside, my heart was too fast. I snorted and the beat sped up. Blaze yelled, "Make it a good time, ladies." The line broke apart, and I thought to go to Jake, receive a kiss, some affirmation. But the men quickly left and I went to the cocaine instead, took my turn, my line, which made my heart fast, faster, happy. All around me, girls checked themselves in mirrors; girls went to their phones and checked themselves there. They made dead faces, glossed mouths open, eyes pointed elsewhere, like they'd been murdered and left. I tried the same look, flipped to see. I looked dead in an ugly way. But it didn't matter, I could practice the pose later.

We would leave the room in heats, Ella announced. While I waited my turn, I did a short line of a sparkly pink powder someone called *2CB*, synthetic cocaine. It made me dance in place for a few minutes, my body like a marionette, compelled. I waited, snorted, danced. I talked to every girl, suddenly social, overeager, my hands fluttering to help: this one with an errant eyelash, this one with her tit tape, this one with her angles. I interlaced my fingers with this one's fingers, took her phone to take her picture, gave her mine and posed, and posted.

"What's your name?" we asked each other and didn't hear the answer.

Ella came with a basket. "It's that time, ladies," she said and we each put our phone in. I saw the basket drop with the weight each girl deposited. They'd be kept safe, Ella said, returned in the morning when the work was done. She smiled and her tooth gap gaped. She paired girls off, a buddy system. She gestured at the girl closest to me, her name already forgotten. "You're a team," she said. We took hands, giddy, and swung them as we walked. Out of the room, down the elevator. Out of the elevator into the crowd of men, which opened up to have us.

18

Girl and I, good at our job. Girl and I chopped by strobe lights, on the dance floor, sucking vape pens, kissing smoke. Girl and I made immortal by our kiss, the cameras, the men who cried out *yes* as if Girl and I were both a game and its players, and they wanted us to win. I had felt sick before, I had felt scared. But now I felt outside all that, like a girl I didn't know.

As we left the room upstairs, Ella had warned us not to get sloppy. We were there to stock the party, give @Chrisss material, make Blaze Cannabis followers hungry from afar. Men were there as Blaze's guests. They were there to indulge in the Product, invest in the Product, buy stock in the future of the Product; they should want what only Blaze could have. They were everywhere, the guests, the men, standing around tables of artisanal glass bongs shaped like assault rifles, standing around cases of Blaze Product, fat green clusters sparkling under glass like engagement diamonds. The men were clean-shaven, baby-faced in jackets sewn with record label patches. They were scruffy in suits with skinny black ties. They wore designer hoodies slung with diamond chains. They wore beanie hats, baseball hats and fedoras. They were watched by security guards, stationed at every exit. And still, the men tried to get us. They waved dime bags and diamond wrist watches, patted breast pockets of Cialis. "Don't worry, baby," they yelled. "Don't be scared."

Girl and I weren't scared. We took our glasses from bartenders and waitstaff only, took our weed from Blaze's pens, our coke and 2CB from twin baggies Girl kept tucked in her bikini top. It wasn't sloppy if it was just us in the bathroom, passing the bags. "Is there anything more timeless than two girls doing blow in a bathroom stall?" Girl said, and offered me her pinkie nail, mounded with powder. I wanted to know her name but was embarrassed to admit I hadn't heard it. I wanted her Instagram handle but our phones were hidden anyway.

"Is this your first time at one of these?" I said and waved my hand to convey the word, "parties." She told me it wasn't. "They're not always this fun," she said.

We moved into the crowd again. The men parted for us. "How you doing, ladies?" they asked and we smiled, sparkled, waved hands, tits, asses, as we were supposed to. On an elevated platform, a DJ in a Nacho Libre mask spun with one hand, waved at the crowd with the other. We danced, returned to the bar, then the bathroom. We moved outside, inside, outside to a ledge. We danced along the lip, the cold pool below, just in case we fell. Behind us, a squat line of decorative fire and @Chrisss's camera, flashing. I felt drunker than before. I hit my angles better than before.

The song changed and Girl and I climbed down, snorted in the open, yelled stories at each other. Girl told me about the man who paid her rent and tuition at an online fashion design school.

"I just feel like I'm destined for more," she yelled.

"The guy I live with bought my tits," I answered and felt immediately ratchet. "I want to go to school," I said. "But my mom is sick." For once her illness didn't feel like an excuse.

"Is she okay?" We were leaned in, Girl's breath hot and stale, but not unpleasant.

"She's really sick," I snapped. Girl's eyes met mine for a moment, then drifted up, to something behind me. Hands closed around my shoulders.

"How you feeling, babe?" Jake asked.

"Hey," I said, and smiled with my teeth.

"You want some pictures with Blaze?"

Girl said, "Fuck yes."

I said, "Absolutely," proud that I could get her chosen.

Jake held my hand, I held Girl's hand. We cut together through the bodies, toward the house. Above the giant door, a man-sized panther head had been illuminated. It glowed, green and furred where night and neon met. Below, Blaze talked to @Chrisss, who flipped through images on his camera. Jake stopped us in front of them.

"These are the girls," Blaze said and then, "Where'd they go?" @Chrisss stepped back and scanned the area. He lifted an arm and gestured at two men, standing bar-side in black and red leather jackets. They returned and @Chrisss arranged us all in a crescent, the men at either edge, arms around Girl and me, Blaze and Jake in the middle. I felt Jake's hand on my waist. Below it, the new man's palm: calloused. Girl felt far away and too fucked up. I waggled my jaw, heard it click.

"Everyone freeze," @Chrisss yelled. The camera shot bursts of light, over in seconds. The man took his hand away. Jake didn't. "Nice," @Chrisss said. He had Girl pose alone, then me.

I was wreathed in neon. I was prostrate at the Rainbow Room, draped over the Las Vegas craps table, then posed over a pool of angry koi. Every image on my grid was in me and from them I knew where to go: gut tucked, elbows in, shoulders out, hips pitched. I sucked Blaze's weed pen and exhaled its vapor, a heavy metal cloud. @Chrisss lowered the camera to see what was good and it was everything. He held the screen for Blaze, who blew smoke at it and nodded. Ella had appeared and looked too. Girl angled toward them all, and I wedged myself between her body and Jake's.

Jake said, "Want to go to the VIP room?" a whisper just for me. I looked at Girl, thought I should stay. "Let me steal you," Jake said, and handed me a drink. I sipped, watched Girl. He tugged my arm. I had perhaps hesitated too long. Because Ella took Girl's hand, whispered in her ear, and they moved in a different direction. I sipped again, felt my legs begin to slur, every step an effort as Jake led me through the party. It parted for us. It tipped, turned sideways. I ditched my glass to hold his hand with both of mine. At the elevators, he nodded to security and they nodded back. Doors parted. We stepped into a silent box. When it lurched to take us down, I fell into Jake and he called me baby, took my face in both hands, kissed it all over. "Where's your drink, baby?" he asked. I couldn't answer, couldn't remember. He propped me in the corner and reached in his pocket for a vial. It had a 😌 sticker on it. He held out the spoon.

"What's that?" I asked and bumped before he answered, something that burned, harsher than 2CB, more chemical than cocaine. I made a face.

"Again," he said. "It'll get you right." Again, I inhaled. My nose closed. When he kissed me, I couldn't breathe.

"Baby, baby," he said and squeezed my breasts, shot with pain. The elevator opened, offered a hallway, dim-lit and long. I put my weight in my heels. "I'm fucked up," I said. The words got halfway out and dropped. Jake pulled my hand a little.

"I got you," he said. "Remember how I take care of you?" Every step counted off in my head. I had to consider where to put my feet. The hall became a hole, the hole became a room. I counted my steps to get inside. Then, I fell.

I felt Jake help me land, felt cushion beneath me. I thought of my phone, thought it was on me somewhere, thought I might remove it from my body, might film the room and find my place inside it. As it was, my phone was upstairs and my eyes had become shutters. I could only see in bars. Other senses turned up. The smell of liquor and coke drip: leather, poisonous flowers. Jake's body, warm, then gone, a cold hole instead of him. The door clicked, soft. I was alone.

I closed my eyes, those shutters, fell further, fought my way back. I opened the shutters and the bars of light had slanted. I heard the door, heard Blaze's voice, and the sound of someone I didn't know. I blinked and couldn't see. I tried to move and couldn't move. Hands clasped around my waist. Dry skin snagged. The grip was hesitant, then sure. The hands flipped me to all fours. I saw the back of a green couch; I saw a handle, the door. I wanted to see the men, who was there, how many of them. But I couldn't manage. I could move my arm and reach, but my fingers closed around empty air. Acrylic tips dug into my palms. I opened my mouth and maybe I screamed. Maybe I tried but no sound came out.

19.

Out of the Princess Suite and into another hotel elevator. I step in and it lifts, pushed upward. I count the dings of every floor, reach into the robe, careful with my fingers, feel the hilt of the steak knife, my dull protector. The doors open and I walk into a hallway, the smell of carpet cleaner, an arrangement of maudlin flowers, the light a jaundiced yellow.

I am not afraid. I storm the hall, bold until I see I've gone the wrong way and scuff back slower. Words and memories cluster in my head. Anesthesia can be like that, spotty with what it erases. The past two nights are foggy to me, but I remember fifteen years ago with greater clarity. I remember the Arizona mansion, the warm clasp of Jake's hand around my hand; I remember the moment I awoke from my first surgery, the implants Jake bought me, 450 cc silicone I've since swapped for grafts of my own fat, harvested from my midsection and "flanks." Which feels purer somehow. My breasts are constructed, but it's all me inside them. All me, only rearranged a little.

The trade—implants for fat—felt, when I made it, like a

final *fuck you* to Jake. My breasts, molded out of my own material, would feel more like mine, I thought. But the fuck you
part didn't last, and only sometimes do I love the abundance
of flesh and fat that took the place of prosthesis. Natural is
better than prosthetic. Natural is moral. Natural connotes a
certain kind of woman, a peaceful wise-woman, a woman like
my mother. This is the logic I've let guilt me, guide me; this is
the woman I've been trying to become. I have long considered
Aesthetica™ the last step in returning myself to this better,
natural state. Even if I could be natural only artificially; even if
I could be natural only in death. But I survived.

I survived, so now what? What will I feel when the swelling
goes down and I see my real face? Can I fight the anesthetic
siren song, the surgeries that promise death and rebirth, a new
untarnished life? Maybe, I think now, fucked up on painkillers and tripping down these hotel halls, past door after door
of possible outcomes, I've been trying to return to a woman I
can never be. I think of that first procedure, before Jake drove
me home and answered my phone, before my mother and all
that mess, I woke for a moment in a recovery room, swam up
to the sound of my own name. Only a nurse was there with
me, calling me. She looked at me a long time, checking something—the light behind my eyes, my movement, my pain. She
asked me how I felt and the answer was: safer than I'd ever felt
before. I felt awash in optimism, joy, pride in my own survival
and a certain clarity about how loved I could be, if I allowed
it. How from such certainty, such allowance and love, I would

speak, sell, grow. Fight, if I had to. Maybe I was wrong. Maybe it was just the drugs, warming me, swaying me. But I've never forgotten that certainty, never stopped trying to return to it, always promising myself that when I get there, I'll find my voice, and use it.

I arrive at a door, powder-blue. The DO NOT DISTURB button is lit up and I stare for a moment at the barrier, imagine rushing in on the man behind it, relentless with my scalpel. With my scalpel, I will teach him what it means to be a woman. I lift a fist, knock softly and feel the blood slosh inside the drains toggled to my head.

I pound. From inside the room, childish cries pick up, high-pitched and pleading.

And then a deeper voice. "Enough," it yells. I return my hands to my pockets, grip the knife, roll my shoulders back. I feel the man behind the closed door. The lock *click-clicks* and the chain makes a noise like chimes. Now is the moment. I finger the blade as Henry opens up. "Lone Star?" he says. I jump across the threshold.

20.

When I woke alone at the Blaze Ranch, it was in a room I had never seen before. The couch I'd been sleeping on was cold leather. A muted TV flashed on the wall in front of me. I sat up too fast, saw black, then blue. Red returned me to the room and I caught my breath, looked for the door and saw it was closed. I heard myself exhale and leaned back. It didn't feel safe, but I couldn't help it, I shut my eyes.

I opened them again and the light was dimmer. I looked down at myself, dressed in a neon green robe I didn't remember finding or choosing. Beneath, I was bare, waxed around my crotch—which was throbbing—tan where I'd been spray painted. I had broken a single green acrylic nail on my left hand, and I squeezed it with my right thumb and pointer finger, relieved when pain sprung up and covered the rest of me, the places that ached, the places still sleeping, pins and needles in my arms and legs like they'd been starved for blood. There was a remote on the cushion next to me and I touched it to unmute the TV screen. "The President tweeted a warning today—" a newscaster said. I pressed mute again and drifted.

When I opened my eyes next, the room was dark, only the TV for light. I cleared my throat and tasted chemical. I swallowed. My whole body reeked, a caustic cleaning agent smell. Drugs, I guessed: the coke I remembered bumping for hours, the pink 2CB. And Jake, the drink he gave me, the elevator he rode with me, the vial he opened, the red light he led me toward. "I got you," he said. "Remember how I take care of you?" I remembered the slam of a door, the glint of its handle, the foreign feel of paralysis as unkind hands flipped me. Had they belonged to one man only, or had there been more? And where had Jake been? I didn't know. I never would. I closed my eyes.

When I woke again it was daylight and the news was different. A banner at the bottom of the TV said *Breaking* and showed the image of a trollish man, a Hollywood muckety-muck, his fat, neckless face covered in a short, pubic beard. Weight announced itself inside me, or next to me, and I felt around, found my phone tucked in the pocket of the robe. Tucked there by me, or by someone else, I didn't know. I opened the screen. Leah had texted "Got seventh" and a selfie with a purple ribbon. I stared, wanting, like maybe the screen was a wall I could move through, Leah on the other side. "How's Naurene?" she'd added. The wall remained: impenetrable. I blinked, reached up and pulled my eyelashes, removed a strip of mink. The screen was a screen and any reply I sent would be the wrong one. I navigated to my photos folder, thinking maybe there were clues there. My phone had been upstairs, locked in the get-ready room all night, but I still expected it to give me answers. I opened the folder and just as fast, closed it. I opened Instagram, then closed it too. If there were answers, I didn't want them. Or was afraid to know them. I pressed my mother's number. "You've reached the cell phone of Naurene Wrey," she said, straight to voicemail. Which I knew to expect. My mom was in the hospital, oblivious to my whereabouts; her phone was on the kitchen table where I'd left it, plugged into her charger. I had put myself in this position. I had wanted to be here. There was something like a sponge in my sternum, full and sogged, pressing. I stood. My legs shook, I had danced so much.

"Where are you?" I texted Jake and then, unsure of what else to say, how to get the answer I needed, I typed, "I'm sick." But my thumb hovered over the send arrow and I waited, carried the phone to the window, a wide rectangle and beyond, desert, disappearing into dark. I pictured myself, barefoot in the robe, attempting escape, rocks and snakes and saguaros in my way. I would be caught, or nature would take me. Not even my mother would know where to look. I deleted the words, the stink of need on them, and lay down on the couch again, forced myself to open my photos. There were the images from hair and makeup: girls with sexy, immobile faces; girls with matching brunette blowouts and mink eyelashes and perky implants and asses. But that was where my phone had been taken. I went to @BlazeCannabis, saw story footage of girls wreathed in vapor and men; men with blunts and glasses of scotch and thick watches that flashed when they gestured *these nuts* at the camera. I scrolled. There was my face by the pool, by the bar, leaving the bathroom with Girl, our eyes red needles. I scrolled a revolving room of mirrors, embedded in every palm, recording, receiving, posting, gathering. I returned to my photo folder, scrolled back in time until I landed on Leah. She was in the candy aisle at H-E-B, blocks of red and orange color behind her. I pinched to see her face, wide open.

She reminded me of an interview I'd read with a famous fashion photographer. Something about how this—vulnerability, childhood, what Leah had—was the special quality he pulled from his subjects. He stripped women bare, he bragged, made them honest. *A trademark smile*, the scout who found me had said of mine, my teeth too big for my mouth. I touched my lips, stared at the screen, trying to remember the scout's name, when Jake's appeared, bubbled in blue. "Baby, you had a rough night," he wrote. "Be right there, 5 mins." Jake would help me remember. Maybe there was a pill for that. I waited. Five minutes, ten, fifteen. The door opened, and Ella passed through.

"Babe, you went too hard," she said, and sat beside me on the couch, touched my hair. "I told you not to get sloppy."

"Where's Jake?" I asked.

"With Blaze. He sent me for now." I pulled away. On the TV, the news showed footage of a zoo, a pack of otters huddled in a corner of their habitat. "Cold Snap!" the banner said. The seasons were changing, and fast. "I need to go home," I said. "My mom is in the hospital."

ELLA SAID THE right things about my mom, showed
the right amount of alarm. She told me to shower, said she'd
get my stuff. I asked after Girl. "I don't know," Ella said. "I'll
try and find her name." I locked myself in the bathroom with
my phone and removed the robe. In the mirror my whole face
sagged, like someone had grabbed me by the jowls and pulled.
I thought of Shonda the Botox Queen; I thought of my mother,
what do you think, just a little tuck? Steam fogged in from the
mirror's edges until it hid my reflection and I stepped into
the shower. The water was warm. I turned it toward hot until
I burned, which felt right, like my skin might rinse off, discard
the evidence of who I'd been before last night, before Jake,
Instagram. I pumped soap from a dispenser on the wall, rubbed
it over my torso with the lightest touch. I felt certain that if I
pressed, I'd find a tumor, pushed up against my skin. I punched
for more soap, moved my hand to my outer labia, which felt
puffy. When I swabbed inside, stinging. I rinsed quick and got
out. My body, when I dried it, looked like something fragile I
had borrowed, broken, glued back together. But my skin was
numb and nerveless.

I came out of the shower in a towel and found Ella, sitting
on the edge of the couch, texting. My backpack was by her feet
and I dropped my phone inside. She had a *Blaze* branded track-
suit for me to wear. "Did you find the girl?" I asked.

"Not yet," she said. "Need underwear?" I told her no,
took the suit back to the bathroom where she couldn't see me
change, then came back out, got my backpack and carried it in

with me. I didn't want to be alone without my phone. I wiped the mirror. Wiggled my jaw. Jake called it gurning, the way your mouth locks up and aches from too much powder. I had been sloppy.

Behind the door Ella said, "Okay, I talked to Blaze, we're getting you out ahead of schedule because of your mom." She would drive me to the airfield herself. "We take care of our girls," she said.

Downstairs the floor was covered in liquid and ash. A group of Buds slouched around in tracksuits like mine. They carried coffee cups and seemed to be waiting. To leave or to stay, it wasn't clear. I looked for Girl among them. But I would never see her again, not on Instagram, not anywhere.

ELLA DROVE ME away from Blaze's mansion, fast like we were both escaping. The road was dark, empty space on either side. She put an elbow on the window, leaned her head on her hand. "Jake's going to call you later," she said. "He's worried about your mom."

I said okay.

"A few things about the party," Ella said. "As you know, all guests sign NDAs upon arrival. Basically, NDAs and the no phone policy ensure that what happens at the ranch stays at the ranch. I sent a copy to your email."

I did and did not understand this as a threat. "Nobody told me what I was signing," I said.

"You should always read what you sign, babe," she said and

then, "My head is literally about to explode." She reached into the back, pulled forward her bag. "Find my Imitrex, will you?" I rifled around in her purse, found the bottle, uncapped it, fed her a pill. She chewed. "Thanks," she said. "I'm sorry you aren't feeling well, either." There was a long silence. "I'm sorry," she repeated. "I'm just fucking tired."

The plane was the same as the day before, the pilot too. I was the only traveler. In the air, Jake called, his voice skipping over words. *Baby*, he said. *Passed out, VIP room, put to bed.* "Can't hear you," I yelled. I threw my phone across the aisle. Then, I unbuckled my seatbelt, got up, retrieved it. I opened my inbox to see the form, scribbled with my eager name, signed the same way I'd walked into Jake's condo, the sex party and surgery suite, the same way I walked through any door: without thought, and with the privilege of thoughtlessness. I scrolled the form's thoughtful language, long, dense paragraphs that meant silence. They meant that if I spoke of the party, the people in it, Blaze could sue me for "injunctive relief," which I understood to mean everything I had. Fractured as his voice had been, I understood Jake was saying that I'd passed out in the VIP, and that the party had ended for me when Blaze found my unconscious, untouched body and sent me to bed.

I didn't believe it. But thought I could choose to.

21.

I wake to cold, conditioned air, the smell of mildew. My mouth tastes the same, smutted. I look around to know where I am. Princess furniture, a neat suitcase full of dark, folded clothes, splayed open on a stand. This is not my room. I almost say it out loud, almost begin to panic, but I glance at the bedspread gathered around my neck, see short bristles of dog hair. And I remember.

I wiggle to an upright seat in bed, and reach as if to touch my forehead, then stop. I already know I'm not fevered with allergy or infection. In the recovery room at the Aesthetica™ center, I made it through the first twenty-four hours, that slim window when infection is most likely. Now, on my own, I've made it through the first forty-eight. I have arrived safely, conclusively, on the other side. I listen for sounds from the bathroom, listen for the dogs. But there's just a short sort of ticking, coming from an air vent. It stops. I close my eyes.

MAYBE SOME PART of me had known I couldn't do it. Even as I stormed toward the room with my fingers wrapped around the knife's hilt, maybe I knew I wouldn't use it. I was incapable of a bloody #MeToo set piece, maybe I always knew that. Or it was simply the sight of Henry, stripped down to his ballooning boxer shorts, elderly skin and salt and pepper chest hair, that stopped me. If it had been Jake, who knows what would have happened. In the moment, I felt myself jump into the room, into Henry's arms, felt the knife fall from my hands and any purpose I had imagined it serving. I heard myself scream, then cry when he caught me, small, frustrated sobs. It felt like falling into another induced slumber. But I was awake, emotional, alert enough despite the drugs.

"Lone Star, is that you?" he asked, and sat me in an armchair, upholstered in slick pleather.

"Oh, it's me," I started, but my voice scratched, catching on cuts made where a tube went down my throat and kept me breathing. "It's me," I finished, quieter. Around my feet, two stout dogs milled, whining. I felt their little tongues on my legs, looked down and saw their fat bodies wiggle. They reminded me of babies, but also of pigs. I opened my palms to them absently, gazed around the room as they licked.

"So now you see," I heard myself say and thought of the knife, whether Henry had watched it fall.

"See what?" He was bent at the waist, trying to corral the dogs, his body unlocking smells: Gillette shaving cream and the clean calendula of the natural deodorant I'd later see propped in the bathroom, next to a ratty toothbrush. "Beto, Bernie," he barked.

"It's fine," I said and reached to wipe my tears, thought better of it. "Just look at me." He hesitated a moment. Then, he stood, turned. Our eyes met. His, feathered around the edges by crow's feet, every wrinkle distinguished and therefore sexual. Whereas mine—already beginning to show, thanks to Aesthetica™—will always be evidence of obsolesce, unwanted-ness. This according to a story that felt further away the longer Henry looked at me, the longer I looked back, each second stripping layers—substances, skin—until we were down to our own naked souls.

"Honey," he said finally. "I'm sorry."

I GET OUT of Henry's bed, find my sandals, wiggle in my feet. And that's when I see the knife. It's positioned blade-in next to a fan of twenty-dollar bills on the coffee table, a note. *Breakfast on me, Lone Star*, it says. *Let's talk later.* There's a phone number, a signature, no xoxo or heart. *You wish*, I think and consider the conversation we might have: the knife that fell from my hand and why it was there in the first place; my mental health, irrational tears and outsized female rage. I consider the violence I thought would satisfy me, the gaze I got instead, less male than human, weathered and soulful and real. How, in the moment, I felt cured by it. Though now, in the light of day, I know that's too tidy to stick. There's no proce-dure, no pill, no person. Salvation is incremental, a smattering of small braveries.

I take the money—a hundred bucks exactly—and head for

the door. I'm almost there when I turn around, go back for the note. Fuck it, maybe I'll call.

BESIDES THE BAR, the Princess Hotel has this one restaurant, separated from the pool by a hedgerow, trimmed in the shape of hoop skirts and hourglass waists. From the other side, a girl screams and I startle, then settle. A cannonball splash ruptures the water. I leave my phone faceup on the table, open a menu, close it when the waiter arrives.

He's got a face like a hangover, slack and purple. Which maybe accounts for why mine—covered by knockoff LV sunglasses, slathered in antibacterial ointment and shrouded in gauze and my sweatshirt's hood—doesn't faze him. I look weird, but not for LA, where cosmetic recovery is a status symbol as much as the work itself. Almost as much as beauty itself.

"Anyone joining you?" the waiter asks and I tell him no, put my hands in my lap while he removes the extra place settings. I watch the knife glint in his hand. It disappears into the pocket of his apron.

"I know what I want," I say, and he says, "shoot."

"Steak, eggs over easy, yes potatoes, yes toast, whole wheat, yes butter."

"Juice?" he asks and reaches to the menu I still hold. I flinch, let go. He flips the stiff page and holds it before me, showing the array of wheatgrass wellness shots and CBD cocktails this place still serves to clueless tourists. That trend died years ago. "Just coffee," I say and choose almond from an assortment of alternative milks. "Got it," he says and goes away. I reach in my pocket, remove the six brown mushroom capsules I took from my room after I left Henry's. I've foregone oxys, muscle relaxers, benzos, in service of a psychedelic trip, and should be in more pain than I am. It surprises me, how good I feel. Groggy, but not hurting. I put the mushrooms on the paper placemat. I sip my water, look around. One table over, a trio of boy children wear Marvel superhero costumes and beg their haggard parents to hurry.

"I've literally taken one bite," the mother says.

"You wanted French toast so better eat up," the dad barks.

Even when I was trying to rebrand, I never wanted kids. I didn't trust myself with the responsibility and was right not to. But now, in this healing place, with the promise of my new appropriate face, responsibility feels possible, pregnancy feels possible, the mommy makeover I'll plan for after feels possible, everything does.

The waiter returns with my coffee, walks off again. I dump in artificial sweetener, make a chemical mound on the surface, watch it sink. He's back with my plate before I've stirred, the service so fast the food can't be good. But I'm starving, I realize, unwrapping my silverware too urgent to count carbs, cals, fat grams, or bother to care. Nearby, the loudest kid douses his toast in syrup. He shrieks when it spills and my head slices open. I cut into my steak, the incision tough and gristly, then fork a bite, shovel in meat to seal myself up again.

It hurts to chew and the food is bland but my brain fizzes

when it meets my mouth, my stomach, cutting the fog of yesterday's journey. I fork with one hand, open Instagram with the other. I check Jake's story, find nothing new and move to my DMs, hoping I'll see a fresh note there, the reporter, so eager to listen. But the messages are all old, already seen. The ball is in my court, now. I navigate away, back to the scroll: Erin, the weightlifter turned direct-sales leggings ambassador has since turned mom and performs for two million viewers an entire at-home workout with only her freshest infant for weight. I watch her lunge and thrust. The baby gurgles when she holds it to her chest and jumps. Some years ago, that Instagram friend of hers climbed to 450,000 followers when her butt got better, then lost 20,000 and a resistance band sponsorship when it turned out to be fake. Erin's ass is definitely real, just smaller, shrunk by trend, I guess. The late nineties-era skin and bones I was born into came back into fashion this decade, lucky for no one. But it'll change again soon, of that I'm certain.

I think of a line from a movie I saw recently. Something about how salesmen never stop speaking long enough to listen. They already know what the customer will say next, what they'll want. They know to anticipate the next vibe shift, next nostalgic cycle. That's why I'm bad at selling. No foresight. I'm always certain that *this* moment, *this* fashion, *this* platform, is the final version, that culture has finally reached its final form and will flatline there. I'm always too busy listening to the customers who come to the black and white striped store for whatever serum I might recommend, always forgetting to upsell, forgetting to give them my name, to walk them to the register and assure my commission, always last place in the monthly sales roundups. Even as @annawrey, I wasn't favored by sponsors. I should have been good enough to win their business and make it my own; my look, my account, that impossible patina—everything that was already soft and pretty Photoshopped to be even softer, prettier, more impossible—should have been what sponsors wanted.

But I was listening when I should have been talking, acting, fighting. I've been this way since girlhood. Before Instagram when there was only Myspace, Facebook, the old capital I-Internet, I was stuck typing terms into Firefox or Safari: "fall fashion," "model blog," the name of whatever celebrity I admired, "Scarlett Johansson," "Megan Fox," women I looked nothing like, had no possibility of resembling. I listened to the culture's silent songs about who was desired and why and I believed them. I believed that Instagram, the filtered aesthetic it popularized—*Instagram face*, we called it—was true. It was how people had always wanted to look, would always want to look: high cheekbones, cut jaw lines, frozen brows, fish lips and perfect symmetry. I thought that was an everlasting ideal. When after some years, it shifted—girls, women, people, going filterless, makeupless, foregoing injectables, drugs, social media itself—I thought the world had changed, that from then on everything would be different. Culture seemed to think so, too. Then the ideal changed once more, as it was always going to.

Today, post pandemic, dictatorship, social justice revolution, anti-wokeness revolution, and everything that followed, Instagram has been made almost obsolete by the next thing. It survives solely thanks to old folks, CGI influencers, and mega-famous, multi-platform content creators like Erin and Jake. We real people are supposed to be beyond aesthetics again. Again, morality is what we're supposed to have arrived at, an obvious, absolute morality we can all agree is right and good, pure and natural. The collective over the individual, the collective over the #cancelleds, the Karens, the ableds, the incels, the long-haul Purells. The collective agreement that only certain stories deserve telling, while others should stay untold, punished for the privilege they once had. Of course, there's always the fact of the self, that complex organism; the fact of the soul which wants to tell itself. At the time I created @annawrey, the most popular soul belonged to a beautiful girl with a dead father and domineering mom, a girl with a heart-shaped face, a sex tape, reality show, celebrity wedding, and slim, ribless waist, giant ass. When she declared she wanted to be a lawyer, to fight for the rights of the wrongly accused, people said it was impossible. But impossible is what we loved her for, followed and paid her for. It was only when she wanted to be smart, useful, that we wondered if she could.

I CHARGE BREAKFAST to the Princess Suite, move the decimal point and double the number like my mother taught me to leave a decent tip. Then I open my phone, call a car. *Arriving in five minutes*, it says, *Look for Gary in the blue Infiniti*. I gather my mushrooms, palm them to my mouth, kill my coffee to swallow them down. They're covered in gel and still I taste the shit they grow in. I walk toward the lobby to wait.

In the light of a new day, filtered by the lavender-orange of my sunglasses, the Princess Hotel looks sweeter than it ever has. I sit in a pink and white selfie throne and watch tourists filter in and out. Some gawk at my incognito outfit as they pass, but not many. Mostly, I'm invisible, blended in with my surroundings: thrones and magic mirrors and me. *It'll be a relief*, my mother said once, *the end of all that being looked at*. She said she wanted it to be just her, no men to show off for and though at the time I didn't believe she meant it, now I suppose I do. Maybe it was the way Henry looked at me, stripped, the way I'd asked him to look, but today there's a sort of contentment to invisibility, even if I suspect it won't last. I suspect I'll recover, return, and sometimes the wanting will, too: to be beautiful, to be seen, to be loved and never left. Desire like that isn't a failure, or a girl-hood flight of fancy. It's a fact of every life.

I reach into both pockets of my hoodie. In one, I feel Henry's cash, the note he left. In the other, I feel my phone. I remove the note, the phone, unlock the screen and save his number. But the sound of men's voices chorusing *sick bro*, and laughing, makes me look up, scan the lobby, think of Jake. My heart begins to pound. It's not impossible that he might be here. We're both in Los Angeles, anything is possible. Nor is it impossible that he might recognize me beneath the shades, the mask, the passing of years that will show up on my skin soon, thanks to Aesthetica™.

The voices come again, *siiiiiiick*. A troupe of teenage boys rounds the corner. They are obviously tourists in their folded baseball hats, wrap-around sunglasses, flip-flops; they are holding up their phones, showing each other screens on which I think I see the faint shape of women's bodies, arranged in desirous postures. I breathe. Stupid of me, to have jumped to Jake, stupid to have forgotten he's aged, too, gone invisible in his own way. Even when we first met, when I was young like these bros, Jake was almost thirty; I never knew him young like them, though he always seemed like it. For an instant, I imagine his current home life, the life of a privileged forty-something white guy: a messy dinner table, free-range red meat and kale salads, organic wine and a wife in a paisley maxi dress calling out the backdoor for her kids to come in. But even my fantasy of the unfiltered Jake feels glossed over and idealized, absent any evidence of his past, the parties and photo stunts, the moments of violence and betrayal I know he's responsible for. Maybe that's why he's often off hunting, holing up alone in the middle of nowhere. Perhaps he's out there meditating on what he did wrong, what he wishes he could take back. It's a sweet fantasy, flavored by smug comeuppance, and I get lost for a moment, imagining Jake's contrition. But the pinging phone in my own hand shakes me back to the real world, the real, probable reality in which Jake is still thoughtless, deserving of a punishment I haven't yet given, and time has still passed and Gary in the blue Infiniti has arrived. He's waiting.

I get up, close the screen, and hurry toward the door. "Have fun, hon," the front desk clerk calls in my wake. Outside, the morning smog has already faded. I walk out into Los Angeles. Bright sun. Jasmine on the air. Ash, and fire.

22.

I returned from the Blaze party in the early morning, changed, and went straight to the hospital. A yellow light warmed the room's appliances, the pink curtain, metal IV stand and beige monitors. My mother's face, that too was cast in the glow. She was awake. And I could see she was alive in a way she hadn't been the day I left. Had she noticed I was gone?

"Hi," she said, and then, "Honey?"

"Mommy," I said and thought I could tell she'd felt lost when she woke without me.

She said, "What are you wearing?" I looked down at the tracksuit, *Blaze Cannabis* embroidered over my heart.

"I'm sorry I wasn't here when you woke up," I said.

"Weren't you?"

I shook my head, both relieved she hadn't noticed and a little disappointed. "Oh well," she said, in the same cadence she said, *you can't have it all*, a phrase she often used.

"You seem better," I said.

"I think"—she shifted in bed, winced—"No, I think I am."

Someone had moved the blue recliner back to the window. I

pulled it close to her again, hung my overnight bag on the back and sat, balled up. My mind flashed to Leah, not three days ago, assuming the same position. *You could stay*, I'd said when I dropped her at the airport. But she had left, so I had also.

"Your mom's such a trooper," Nancy the nurse said, arriving with a thimble of pills, a cup of water. She handed my mom the thimble, watched her toss it back. "Just a little sip," she said and gave her the water. My mom swallowed, touched her throat, turned to me. "Have you eaten anything lately?" she asked. I hadn't eaten since the two peaches the day before.

"I can bring in a sandwich," Nancy said.

"I'm worried about her," my mom said.

"Of course you are," Nancy said. "You're a good mom, she's a good girl."

Something like pride touched my mom's face. Something like a curtain began to lower.

"How's your pain?" Nancy asked.

"Better now," my mom said and turned to me. "How was it seeing Leah?" The question melted, dribbled out, and though I wanted to answer, to sit on the side of her bed and wonder at the differences between my little girl twin and me, the small ways in which we remained the same, I could tell my mother wasn't up for it. She would disappoint me if I tried to talk, and I didn't think I could take it.

"I'll check on you girls in a while," Nancy said.

"Do you need anything?" my mom asked me again, like if I did, I should place an order. Like I might take whatever pill she had, and together we might rest. Nancy was already out the door.

"Mom," I said, "worry about yourself." My words sounded tight and plucked. "Just sleep." She had to fight not to. "I'm going to let you sleep." I wandered into the hall. Nancy was around the corner, typing into a monitor on a wheeled platform.

"Is she sleeping?" she asked and I told her, "Just."

"Are you?"

"Not really," I said, and surprised myself with both the truth, and its evasion.

"Why don't you go home? I'm the one working a double."

"Can I stay?"

"I'm not going to kick you out again," she said and walked me to a kitchenette, showed me the coffee maker, a mini fridge stocked with puddings and saran-wrapped sandwiches. I ate. And I did sleep, next to my mother in the blue recliner, dreamless.

THE NEXT AFTERNOON, Nancy showed me how to help my mom out of bed and sit her on the toilet. She peed, which was progress, and Nancy showed me how to lift her off the bowl. After, my mom was tired, and slept. I counted my Xanax, found three pills left, swallowed one. I sat in the blue chair and watched TV, my phone, the door. I moved around my mind, routine. I was fine, we would be fine. I would wait and she would wake and we would walk to the nurse's station and back, my arm around her.

It happened just like that, my mother's body in mine, our synched-up steps. "I'm so much better," she said as we shuffled. I squeezed her waist a little, which was soft where I held it, and warm. The man, or men, their hands had been dry. It was impossible to tell her how they'd felt. "I'm almost there," she said as we neared the nurse's station. "I'm coming back," she said when we turned and retraced our steps. Nancy waited at the door and clapped. Together we got to the bed, velcroed on compression socks, untangled wires.

"I'm going home, kissing my kids, watching *The Bachelor* and sleeping," Nancy said, and told me to go, too. I followed her orders like a test. "I'm coming back," I told my mom before I left. But she was already asleep and didn't answer.

FROM THE DRIVEWAY, the cottage looked braced for weather, shuttered and dark. I walked to the door with my house key held out in front of me. I considered the lock as I turned it. Inside, I went room to room, checked closets, turned on every light. I was alone, but showered with the curtain open, watching the door, watching the water spill out. The spray tan I'd received for the party was peeling. I turned the tap all the way toward hot and scrubbed with my acrylics. Orange flakes melted off and I kicked them down the basin to the drain. No, I couldn't tell my mother what happened. Away from her, I could hardly breathe. I got dressed, packed my stuff into her purse, got back in the car.

"She's so much better today," I texted Leah. She replied 🖤

🖤🖤. My mom, when I returned to her room, was as I'd left her: sleeping. I put myself beside her, eyes on the door, keeping watch.

THE BLUE RECLINER was like a safe zone in a child's game; its embrace turned me untouchable, so sleep took me away again. To a familiar nightmare, that collective dream of girls and women: faceless men hunting us, finding us where we hide. I ran, but my feet were weighted. I screamed, but no sound came out.

I WOKE WITH a jolt, to a man's voice at the door, saying *excuse me?* I coughed, felt sweat flood my armpits and chest. It was a delivery guy, arm around an obscene bouquet of flowers.

"Did I scare you?" He held up the bouquet. "Where should I put these?" I pointed at a table near the bed.

"Are those for me?" I asked. Were they from Leah? For me and Naurene both? The beginning of a new togetherness? The man read the card, confirmed my name.

My mother woke. "Look at this," she said in her drug voice, all the spit sucked out.

"Who sent them, though?" I asked.

The man tiptoed into the room, set the flowers on a side table, shrugged. "It's on the card," he said and hurried out like he might catch cancer if he lingered.

"Check the card," my mom said, rifling around her sheets for the pain bolus.

I walked over to the vase, found the card. It was matte black with a silver *Get Well* on the front. Leah wouldn't have picked black, no. I flipped it over. *Sending healing vibes. Love, Jake.* Blood rushed from my head to my guts. My mom said, "From who?" I considered lying, then repeated the message out loud.

"Is this the man who does your Instagram?"

"My manager," I said.

"Your manager," she said, "fancy." Her voice was full, like he was her man, too. I glared at her. Yesterday her face had been pale, but clear. Today, ruddy circles rouged her cheeks.

"Water," she said.

"Little sips," I said and held a cup to her mouth. She drank. When she drifted back to sleep, I took the vase from the table and carried it past the nurse's station, which was empty, through the doors and into the women's restroom. I emptied the water in the sink. It smelled like rotting food and I ran the tap to rinse it down, then dumped the flowers in the narrow trashcan, left the vase on the floor. I returned to my chair, watched *Housewives* on the muted TV.

"Where are my flowers?" my mother said when she woke.

"They were full of bugs," I said, eyes still on the screen, the fighting women, toddling in their Louboutins.

"Such a shame," she said.

I helped her out of bed, held the butt of her nightgown closed, and together we walked the hall and back, no nurse required. My mother pushed her IV stand like a rolling torch, lighting our way.

IT WAS THEN that she started to insist.

"Home is where I'll heal," she said.

"I couldn't agree with you more," Nancy said. My mother's surgeon came by, flipped pages on a clipboard.

"We've been up and walking," I said and felt like a suck-up.

"Remarkable," he said, looking at me, his gaze hard in a way I had learned to recognize, and use.

"I'd love to go home," my mom told him.

"Seems a tad premature," he said, still looking at me.

"I'll take care of her," I said and leaned forward, shoulders back. I smiled my trademark smile and he smiled back. "Let's see what we can do."

The sooner we could start chemotherapy the better, he said. A chemical protocol would really clean her out. And then we could live life to the fullest. Travel, he said. Fun, adventure, bucket list. But first she would need to eat, poop, rest. Anesthesia, surgery, opioids, they shut a body down. Hers would have to work a little harder before the surgeon would let her go home, before he would let her come back and fight.

She chose oatmeal for her first meal, took it in tender bites. I opened my phone to film. Look at my brave warrior mother #survivor, bunny filtered and funny in the midst of misfortune. But seeing her this way made me close the screen, tuck it away. I wanted her to stay only mine. I slept again in the recliner and in the morning she sat on the toilet, determined to go. Eventually she did and I brought Nancy in to bear witness to the proof. A social worker came next and ran my mom's insurance, which wouldn't cover a visiting nurse.

"Are you sure you can handle this, honey?" Nancy asked me.

"I can handle it," I said.

At H-E-B I picked up my mom's prescriptions, Ziploc bags of the heaviest hitters, and no one looked at my ID. I filled a cart with what I wanted her to want. More oatmeal, fiber powder, chicken noodle soup and saltines and ginger ale. Aisle by aisle, I alternated selves. Here I am a woman, shopping, caretaking. Here I am a girl in shock and all the men can tell. They watched me read labels, compare prices, like they knew it was an act. I paid with my mom's Visa, signed with her name. I loaded her car, stopped for gas at the supermarket pump. I used the squeegee to scrub away the grackle crap. I texted Leah, "She's heading home!!" She was healing and so was I.

It was autumn by then, but Texas was still hot. At home, I watched Instagram stories while I went through my mother's drawers, looking for light drawstring pants, a thin zip-up sweatshirt, slide-on flats with rhinestone spackled toes. On the screen, Ella boarded a plane, flew home to LA. Erin shared recent #bootygainz and an entire day of eating. Jake shared bouncing footage of the party, asses and tits and faces hidden by vaporous clouds. He was somehow immune from the no phone rule and I hated him for it. What would have changed if I'd had my phone? I'd know what happened. I closed his story and hoped he'd see I dropped off halfway through.

In preparation for my mother's return, I arranged a pillow

station on the couch for her daytime resting. I put clean sheets on her bed, turned them down to make a triangle of fresh white where she would sit before she lay each night. I opened the Ziplocs, removed every bottle. Ativan, Zofran, Amoxicillin, hydromorphone, patches of fentanyl to alternate with the pills when the pain broke through. Nancy had taught me the routine, extra careful with the patches, latex gloves before I peeled.

I arranged the medications on my mom's nightstand. I filled a glass halfway with water and put it beside the bottles. I brought items like a bowerbird: a tissue box and scented candle; a pumice stone and nail file; a hairbrush. I checked my phone, swiped away notifications, Jake's name. I swallowed my last Xanax and chucked the bottle.

23.

Afternoon, my mom up and ready. Nancy was off, a new nurse on. "Big day," the nurse said and removed the IV from my mother's hand. *Homeward bound*, my mom sang, off key. The nurse helped her to the recliner. "I got it," I said, and stepped in with the outfit I'd picked. My mom and I worked together. Underwear, pants, hoodie. Her body was familiar, but it made no sense why. Before the day I helped her pee, it had been years since I'd seen her naked. She kept the sticky hospital socks, slid haltingly into her rhinestone shoes. Her hair was matted from so much pillow-time.

"We'll fix that at home," I said.

"We'll have a spa day," she said.

The nurse said, "Y'all are cute," and wheeled over a chair.

"I can walk," my mom said, but it was policy for her to ride. I went to the garage ahead of her, pulled the car to the entrance where she waited, seated, an orderly at the helm of her chair. He lowered her into the passenger seat.

"Feel better, girls," he said.

My mother said, "We're free."

"OUCH," SHE HAD said with every struck pothole, for as long as I could remember. But on the way home from the hospital, she was quiet. I turned up the radio, NPR soundbites, *Make America Great Again*, and the swell of a chanting crowd: *USA USA USA*. My mom reached over, pressed the CD button. Aaron Copland, her favorite Americana, swelled from the speakers and she sat up in her chair for him. But she stayed quiet, and by the time we got home, she'd lilted into the seatbelt. "We're here," I said to wake her. She reached slowly for the door handle. "Stop," I yelled. "Let me get it." I ran around, opened her door and kneeled in the frame. "You have to let me help you," I said. "Or this isn't going to work." Her face dropped. "Sorry," I said.

"No," she said, "you're right." I offered her my arms, braced, lifted. She took the porch steps one by one and with the same right foot. I opened the door, held her arm through the kitchen. "Want to try the couch?" I asked. She pointed to her room. "How nice," she said. It was the sheets; she had noticed that I'd folded them, as I'd hoped she would. I helped her sit on the bed and kick her shoes off. She slid one foot under the covers, then the next.

"I made it," she said. "And now I need a pill."

"Didn't you have one before you left?"

"Don't start with that." She closed her eyes, and I swallowed the rush of heat rising up my throat. I wanted to be careful, not cruel. My mother was an addict. "An addictive mind," she said of hers and told me to be careful, too. I went back to the car, got her purse, my phone. I went to the kitchen, washed my hands, counted as I soaped. With a pill already inside her she could only take the fentanyl. It seemed like a reasonable compromise. I pulled two blue gloves roughly from their paper dispenser, snapped them on. I was Shonda, Botox Queen. I was Dr. Holle. I could make a body better. I unboxed a patch, considered cutting it in half, which Nancy had said was an option. I left it whole. In my mother's room, I alcohol-swabbed the skin on her arm where it would go, fanned it dry. She watched, wordless. I peeled the patch. Goo separated from plastic backing. I pressed it to her.

"That'll hold a long time," I said. "Don't ask me for more."

"I won't," she said, and slept so soon.

I TOOK MY phone to the pillow throne I had built on the couch. I could hear her snoring through the wall and turned on the TV to cover the sound. I made it louder to block the squeak and shatter I imagined the front door would make, broken by a strange man's hand. Outside, the sun had set. Across the room, my reflection in the windowpane was haloed by the flat-screen's white glow, the story of a gown, the woman wrapped up inside its feathers and lace.

I've found the one, she cried. *This is the dress I've dreamed of my entire life.* She twirled and clapped her hands. Her mother fluffed the train, wiped tears.

In Ella's new story, she posed with a honeybee perched on the pad of her thumb. Restrained by forceps, the bee inserted its stinger. "Ouch," Ella said offscreen, but her voice was hopeful. "This little guy gave his life so I can feel better," she said. The story shifted to more of Jake's gonzo footage from the Blaze party. Music thumped, weed smoke hung over everything. Soon, official content would post, high production value, Blaze the man edited into a starring role. Maybe I would be there, too. Maybe I'd be cut out. I'd signed, so they could do anything they wanted with me. I shut the phone. The TV played a trailer for a series called *Swamp Rats*. Men in camo baited a human-sized hook with bloody organ meat. *A gator this size*, they said, *is a silent killer, an extreme danger.* At this point, Jake should know not to include me in the official content. I'd ignored him since he led me into the dark, left me and lied about it. I was most afraid of being left, and Jake had left me. The man's hands had been dry and that was where my memory stopped.

I went to the door of my mother's room. She was where I'd left her. Under the sheets I had turned down, under the hoodie I'd zipped, her rib cage rose and fell like a bellows. Her snores were ragged. She was exhausted. Most likely it was exhaustion. She needed rest. Everyone at the hospital had said so. "Mom," I said, and touched her shoulder. "Mom." Nothing changed. "Naurene," I said and shook her a little. She opened her eyes. Her pupils were seeds, grown over the iris. Jake's pupils sometimes looked like that. Probably mine did too. It was the drugs. She turned her face away and I glanced at the bottles of pills, the box of patches, 2.1 mg of fentanyl, the same poison Jake tested his powders for.

"Mom," I said, "wake up." I shook her shoulder again then patted her face. "Naurene," I said, and patted it harder. Her skin was damp, hot. "Stay awake."

Get her strength up, Nancy had said. *Travel, fun, bucket list*, said the surgeon. With rest she might get there, but here I was, forcing her to stay with me.

"I need you awake for a minute," I said, and googled "Fentanyl OD." Slow heart, I read, slow breath, dilated eyes.

"Let me check your heart," I said, and tried to find its beat. Her wrist was quiet. I put my head on her chest, heard a fast, liquid pulse. I read my phone. Cold skin, it said, but hers was burning. I touched her again. Maybe she was only warm and I was the cold one.

"Honey," she said, "I'm just tired."

Her skin looked thin and purple, like it needed to molt and come back better. I didn't want to overreact but dialed 911 anyway, relayed the story. My voice was full of excuses, guilty like a killer.

"I just know there's something wrong with her," I said.

"Has the patient taken any drugs?" the operator asked. I told her what I gave.

"Anything you might not know about?" she said.

"Mom," I said, "did you take anything?" She drifted. I yelled, "Mom, did you take anything?"

"No," she said. "Let me sleep."

"She says no," I said into the phone, and heard the start of my own suspicion.

The ambulance would be right there. I should stay on the line. But I hung up. "I should never have left these here," I said, and gathered up the bottles. I took them to the kitchen and dumped them in a plastic shopping bag like I might need to bring her medication to the hospital. I didn't want the paramedics to see how careless I'd been with it, was the truth.

"I WAS CAREFUL," I told the team of men when they barged in with a stretcher. Outside, red and blue lights moved in circles. "Naloxone," someone said and then, "temperature 104, she's not ODing,"

"Ma'am," they yelled. I stood in the doorframe, craned to see them work. "Heart rate 93." They were broad or they were tall. One on either side of her, and the transfer from bed to stretcher was seamless. "Should I ride with you?" I asked and no one answered. I took her purse, my phone, her keys. I followed the men out the door.

24

"You can't be here," a nurse said. My mother was on a gurney, chaos in rings around her. A new IV, wires clipped to her fingertips, her pulse in frantic beeps. The nurse walked me to a narrow room.

It was not a room for waiting, no other people, no television or magazines, no window, just chairs. I sat, looked at my Instagram: bodies in postures of surprise, love, comfort; bodies sharing discount codes, bodies selling shapewear and period panties, skin routines, name necklaces, magnetic eyelashes, lip plumper, bronzer, the perfect all-purpose skillet. People are so shitty, I thought, and imagined posting a video of the airless room, just me inside, a performance of the empty rooms inside us all. Or posting a video of the room like the most basic bitch, talking to the camera, pleading for sympathy, while her mother fought for life. I imagined telling followers how I'd peeled the patch, applied it to her skin. "I killed her," I would say and go viral, the world rushing to punish or console.

The door opened and a social worker came with admittance paperwork, questions about my mother's history. She would check on me soon, she said, and left. I stared at the pages, dug around in my mom's purse for her driver's license, copied the number. I did the same with her insurance card. I did my best with the rest of her story; the first diagnosis, the surgery in which bones were cut and tumors removed. The leftover holes were filled with special cement. But she still felt them, spaces of ache and absence. This is how she explained the pain.

Halfway down the forms, my phone lit up. I followed it. To a picture tagged by Blaze and posted to his personal account.

The picture was of me, no Girl, no Jake or faceless men. I pinched the screen to see. The expressionless shine of my forehead, the outlines of my implants, the vape pen I forked with my fingers. Smoke funneled in a conical cloud from my mouth and all around, neon light cast a filtered sheen. The picture was a message and only I could read it: I was special. And that was why I had been chosen, shown to the world who saw—

@steveooo912: 🔥🔥🔥
@Kelliegel_: Fine as wine 🍷💀
@A.design17: @BlazeCannabis girls are the hottesssst
@cassandrawins: STUNNING 😍😍😍💋💋
@earthgrab: Bellissima principessa ti amo
@skincareg: Photoshopped
@marinabern: a perfect storm 🔥🔥🔥
@tsimolova: Beautiful
@guy.hilal97: Get Hard to Last Longer 🚀🚀🚀

@patricialocc: MAKEUP GOALZ
@alamedamai: Muahhhh sexxxxo

I moved to my own account, ordained by Blaze, and growing. 80,000 followers, 85,000, 90,000. From a narrow, windowless room, I watched them build, bought by the surgical perfection of my body, the failure of my mother's, as if any love I earned was both a trade and a punishment.

The social worker opened the door, put her head into the room. I jumped, settled, shut the phone.

"I have the papers," I said and held them out.

"I have your mother's doctor here," she said.

The doctor, surgeon, decision maker. His white coat, blue scrubs, stubble. Just yesterday he'd looked at me, my trademark smile, and agreed to let my mother go. I stood, put out my hand for him to shake. I could see he didn't want to. In my palm, his palm was limp. "I'm so sorry to tell you," he said, and the room turned smaller. "There was, at some point, contamination," he said. "In surgery or aftercare, we can't know."

"Okay," I said and started to ask next steps.

He interrupted. "By the time we got to your mother, the infection had progressed. We can't say why this sometimes happens when a patient is sent home."

"What is it you're telling me?" I said.

"I'm sorry," he said. "We couldn't get a hold," and the room became a crowd, too big and close. I counted seconds in my head to stay inside it. One one hundred, two one hundred, three one hundred. I was supposed to stay alert inside it. I looked down at my phone, then up again. I heard myself speak. "Wait, she's dead?"

"How can we help you?" the social worker said. "Is there someone we can call?"

The doctor gave me his business card. The social worker went for water, came back with a nurse, who offered me a Valium and told me to sit down.

I sat, swallowed the pill. My mouth was dry but the water wasn't right in it. "What happens now," I heard myself ask. I looked at the cup. It didn't shake in my hand. It should have shaken. I should have fainted or fallen. My failure to do so meant I didn't love, hadn't loved. The women in the room with me would see my failure and know the truth about me.

"I have some forms for you," the social worker said. I tried again to give her the ones I'd filled out, a child offering a toy to an adult who didn't need it.

"Not those," she said, and something about advance directives.

"What does that mean?" I asked. She told me, but it meant nothing. She said, "If you'd like to see your mother, now is the time." I stood, carried my phone, buzzing. I wasn't thinking, I was only following, walking behind the women to a curtained cubicle. I felt the Valium start its seep, up to my chest where the breath was trapped. "Ready?" the nurse said. I need to see, I thought, and nodded.

My mother was alone. She was alone.

"What the fuck," I said. The nurse was quiet, the social worker was quiet. "Fuck," I said through a kind of crying. "I'm sorry," I said.

"Now is when we ask if you'd like a priest or rabbi," the social worker said.

"I don't know," I said. "No."

She brought me a plastic bag. In it was the hoodie I had zipped, the pants and hospital socks.

"I don't want these," I said but they told me to keep them, so I did.

I WALKED ALONE to the ER parking lot, opened the car door, sat in the driver's seat. I said the time aloud, 5:07 A.M. Not a whole day since she had sat beside me. "We're free," she had said, infection at work inside her. *5:07 a.m.*, I said again because I had read it was a trick, to see if you were dreaming. In dreams there is no time, something like that. But I spoke the numbers and didn't wake up. I pressed the button to start her car.

In the wind of a coming storm, stoplights swung like they might let go, jump. I pulled in the driveway just before the rain. The house was lit up and unlocked. Men's boot prints over the threshold, and all around her bed. Her bed where she had slept too deep. Her water glass. Her pills, the patch, which had not killed her. Her pumice stone and nail polish. I had imagined I would slough dead skin from her heels, shave her legs, brush her hair. I thought I would make up for how I'd left her by measuring meds, counting every forward step she made, using my Blaze money to pay off her hospital stay and take her somewhere new, somewhere she had always wanted to travel. I had imagined this would salvage something, the start of a new story. Instead, I had slapped her. *Did you take anything?* I had yelled. It was the last thing I said before the men came and took her, wasn't it?

I peed and thought, I'm peeing and she's dead. I washed my hands and the thought repeated. Every surface I touched, every room I checked, echoed without her. Rain hit the windows in streaks. I took off my shoes and climbed into her bed, put myself where she had been, put my phone on her nightstand, reached for her pills. I shook out two Dilaudid, swallowed with her water, listened to the storm until the pills dissolved and I slept.

TO THE SAME impossible world, I woke. I was alone. I was 100,000 followers. I was 30,000 hearts, two hundred and eighty-eight DMs. I watched the screen where they lived, but I didn't read the messages they left there. Instead, I killed my mother's water, googled her pills, shook out an Ativan, and swallowed. And waited, scrolling my photos folder to get back to Leah, her candy aisle smile, stripped and open; in the last image, her guarded, sexy pout. I remembered how it had angered me, to see her find the expression, and wear it.

I opened Facetune and went to work on her picture. I left her waist as it was but developed her hips. I snatched her jawline, made her skin matte, her lips fuller, her eyes fox-wide and whiter. I arranged the final image in the square of a fresh Instagram post. For a caption I wrote: "BEST FRIEND FOR-EVER! Follow @LeahReid #bestie." I shared. The Ativan kicked in and I slept. When I woke, Leah's account, chosen by mine, had grown from 365 followers, to 2,700. "Dude, my Instagram is blowing up," she had texted. "My gift to you," I typed but didn't send. I couldn't bear to omit the truth or to tell it. Instead, I composed a message to Jake. "Hey," is all I wrote. "Baby," he replied, "come back."

That was how I left again.

25.

In the Princess Hotel parking lot, a princess-shaped sign points to where the rideshares wait. There, Gary's blue Infiniti idles for me. I try to take the front seat, but it's full: a lunchbox, a basket of gum and granola bars and mini water bottles. I get in the back. "May I offer you—" Gary says. He holds the basket out to me with one hand, steers with the other. I reach, see my fingers hover like they belong to a child, choosing Halloween candy from a welcoming bowl. I consider chocolate, remove a wintergreen lifesaver. The mint feels right on my stomach, which has started to twist. From far away, Jake's voice returns to me: "Shrooms are hard on the gut, but like, profound." Like mirrors, he said, they show us to ourselves. About which, I should probably believe him.

Gary follows a series of signs to the Fairy Tale Land theme park. "Have fun, young lady," he says as I get out. I thank him, slam the door. It shimmers with the sound and the window's tint reflects me, hidden by my hoodie, my mask and sunglasses. I wonder how Gary knows to say *young lady*; I could be anyone. But he's gone too soon to ask.

Families mill around the drop-off area, performing themselves. Escalators zigzag to the entrance. I descend, stand in line, use Henry's cash to buy a day pass. A guard checks my bag, my pockets, Henry's note the only item in them. I consider it a moment, then toss it in a trash bin.

"Medical devices," I say to explain the drains behind my ears, hidden by the sweatshirt's hood.

The security guard waves a wand around my head.

"All good," he says. I walk into a new world.

AFTER MY MOTHER died, I couldn't be alone. The Blaze events were crowds to disappear inside and where once this might have scared me, as an orphan, I was grateful. The second party I attended was smaller than Arizona, and secret, designed less to court investors than to cater to men who'd already bought in. It was held in a house on Franklin Boulevard, where the Black Dahlia was rumored to have been killed. "In the basement, before the guy cut her in half and posed her like a Picasso," Blaze said when he gave guests the grand tour. He opened the cellar door, pointed out wooden steps stretching into a darkness girls peered down. "Just a rumor," he said, and shut the door again.

Everyone left their phones at coat check. Everyone signed NDAs. Jake paired me off again, like we'd agreed to it. Which maybe I had. Maybe my return after the Arizona party was another passed test, another contract signed, eight grand for one night and the promise of more to come. At the Black

Dahlia house, the man Jake introduced me to was forty-five, fifty, but dressed as a skater boy, silver-headed beneath his stiff Thrasher hat. I took his hand. I was sober and didn't have to be convinced. I wanted to remember what I did with the man, wanted to control the part of the story that came after, with the morning light. I remember best how many rooms there were to choose from, how ours was purple-walled, furnished to match. I remember how fast my time there went, how I left my body as if in sleep, how my body did for itself what anesthesia does, and floated off for a while. I woke to see the man, standing over me, finishing himself. He wiped with a Kleenex. We returned together to the crowd below. Later, I saw him climb the stairs with another, younger girl.

After that, Jake sent Ella and me to Shonda for Sculptra butt injections because "slim thick" bodies were the newest ideal I didn't quite match up to. Blaze Cannabis picked me for an ad campaign, shot by @Chrisss of course. The product was for sex, CBD dominant lubes and tinctures and sublingual tabs promised to boost libido. In the final image, posted to the company socials and featured for a month on a billboard at Santa Monica and Vine, I was almost an afterthought, seated on the edge of a bed in the shadow of a man, buttoning or unbuttoning his dress shirt. I could imagine rush hour drivers turning down news coverage of the #MeToo moment, to look up at me and shake their heads. "What a cultural mindfuck," they would say. Or else they'd say nothing, just take me in with the exhaust of five o'clock traffic. I couldn't imagine anyone wanting what I sold. But I posted the billboard to my followers, tagged @BlazeCannabis. "Gonna be a big staaaah," I wrote and received endless empty hearts in response. "I love you so much," followers wrote. "ur my idol," they promised. But what did they know of idols and love? Everything, nothing, just like me.

DURING THIS TIME, I stayed with Jake, let my mother's house in Houston sit, no boards on the windows, even. I let Jake keep paying. He set me up with men sometimes, who also paid. We kept fucking, though fucking had become an empty, sensationless space in which I thought about other things. Sometimes I thought about my mother, but only for an instant before I covered her with something else, visions of body modifications, mostly, plans for what technology I could try next: CoolSculpting, EmSculpting, AirSculpting, laser facials and hair removal, a buccal fat facelift, a Nefertiti neck lift, cheek implants, jaw implants, temple filler, tear trough filler, filler for my marionette lines. I chose scalpels, needles, lasers to inflict the pain I deserved, the transformation, the healing. Sometimes they worked. Mostly, they didn't.

　　Procedure by procedure, month by month by year, Leah became a distance, especially after I told her about my mom, watched her grieve and wondered why I couldn't. What was it about me that failed to feel what I was supposed to? I didn't want to feel it; I wanted to be forced to feel it, as if feeling would prove the love I'd had, squandered, lost for good.

Two years after my mother's death, Leah started seeing someone, another runner. He had 60,000 followers and when they went Instagram official, Leah's grew too. He wore leggings under wind shorts and was always moving. They wanted to start a gym together, she said, selfie mode, in her stories. It was their dream. "He pushes me to be better," she wrote when we texted. In the images she posted, she looked thinner than before. It hardly seemed possible. But everything is an illusion. Jake's words, not mine. Jake's words, and Ella's.

"I gave the illusion of perfection, but I knew there was something wrong with me," Ella told her followers, last post before the surgery that returned her to herself. Return is another word of hers, spoken from a hospital bed, recovery. "I've been returned to myself. I wouldn't have known how to get here if it wasn't for social media. Social media saved me. Other women's stories, #breastimplantillness and its three hundred thousand tags, saved me. I'm telling you girls, explant now."

Her immune system had been attacking her implants, she said. Every symptom she experienced was a side effect of her body's war with the silicone it carried. So, she excised the source, returned to herself, urged others to do the same with a vehemence that scared me. Natural is better, she said. Natural is right and good. I believed her, but not wholly. Had she been less sure her sickness belonged to other women, too, I would have believed her more. As it was, she was certain in a way that felt suspect and I kept my implants until I traded them for fat, and never did I think they made me sick, not literally. But the story of Ella's rebirth, her new, natural life, is the story thirteen million women follow her for; her story and the following it won her, has eclipsed Jake, Blaze, the mess of her past; she has been delivered so surely from sickness to stardom.

INSIDE THE PARK, people dress as characters from fairy tales: goblins and dwarves, evil queens and princesses. On mushrooms they look realer, everything does. Everything feels closer, the tourists who mill around gift shops stuffed with reaching color. The food carts and roller coasters with three-hour wait times. The screams as riders rise and plummet. I walk past the big Billy Goats Gruff ride, and through the Jack and the Beanstalk Experience where everything is giant. I focus on the turrets and spires of a distant castle, its single lonely tower puncturing the sky. The closer I come, the less I see, but magical theme music lifts up, mixed with phone pings, baby cries and laughter, the noise of other worlds. I'm daunted, and thinking it was a mistake to dose myself here. I expected epiphany, but so far all I feel is awkward and the only realization I've come to is how similar the paved and painted world around me is to nature. I pass under an archway, enter a pretend village where pretend peasants barter and where, I suppose, heroes and heroines are supposed to have grown up, never guessing they were special until adventure presented itself and they denied, then finally accepted, the call. Or maybe they always knew they were special, but hid themselves among the plebes anyway, aware of bad prophecies, jealous step-mothers, violent husbands, the danger in being seen.

I don't know the story. I do know where I want to go but not how to get there. From an unguarded kiosk I take a map, accordion it open before me. The page blurs. I blink to focus and the map clears, but the crowd before me obscures its land-marks and I feel for a moment like a lost child, swallowed by fear and confusion. I walk forward anyway, into a warm morass of skin and sweat and excitement. I pass carts selling crowns and scepters, glass slippers and candy that tastes like honey-dew nectar, ambrosia, air, whatever it is that fairy folk eat. Kids point Fairy Tale Land branded interactive devices—swords and wands, mostly—at frozen screens and animatronic diora-mas until curses break, pixels rearrange, figurines move and beasts become men again, frogs become princes, sleeping prin-cesses awaken and remember where they are.

"First we get my wand," a child sings from somewhere up ahead. "Then we go to all the magic places." I point myself in the direction of her voice.

THE THIRD BLAZE party I attended was big again, back at the Arizona mansion and lorded over by a famous DJ duo credited with house songs that sampled nameless wom-en's voices. It was Christmastime. I overfilled my lips for the occasion, painted them red and donned the sexy Santa cos-tume all the Blazed Buds had to wear. I woke two days later in an unmade bed, no memory of the night, the man, the men, whatever pill I'd been given to disappear so long. There were bruises on my thighs. There was cash on the coffee table, crisp bills like the ones Henry would leave, only more of them. And just like Henry's money, I took it. But I had lost control of my story. Back in LA, I woke angry in the night, packed Jake's stash and returned to Houston, telling myself this gave me power. In Houston I would get myself together. Another story I decided to believe. I would use Instagram for sponsorships, the way I'd always meant to, the way Jake had promised I could. I would sit at a hotel bar, advertise on backpagepro, start an OnlyFans, DM rich guys, whatever it took to assemble a network of protection and support, no Jake required. But the cottage I returned to was not what I expected. Four years gone by, everything mildewed, only myself to blame; I had left it all to rot.

I drove to H-E-B, bought "Texas Strong" trash bags, a bottle of white wine, a rotisserie chicken I craved abruptly and with feral force. At home I split the bird, ate from its open body. I bagged the contents of my mother's closet, damp and mossed. I bagged the expired pantry. I scooped unused toiletries from drawers I wanted empty, all traces of her erased.

"Fucking unacceptable Anna," Jake texted after I ghosted. But what could he do? Well, I never worked again, not for brands as big as Blaze. This shouldn't have surprised me, but it did. I was surprised to be reduced to sponsorships for hair-thickening serums, diet tea, waist trainers, which I found by replying to old comments, offering to "collab." Each product paid around five hundred a post, one post a month, a pittance and on top of that, I was bad at selling. I dated a few men, some who paid and some who did not, all of whom dumped me. Always, I was surprised to be alone. Maybe I brought it on myself. Certainly I took the pills by myself, the last of Jake's stash, mashed up with my mother's leftovers: two 10 mg Vicodin, two 2 mg Xanax, swallowed with a glass of Pinot gris. In a blackout, I got in my mother's Prius. In a wreck I woke, plastic and steel wrapped around me like a broken hand. My own hand hung from the bone, the wrist snapped twice, reset by a surgeon who chuckled when I screamed. "I wish I got that response from all women," he said. There's no safe way to reject a man; I laughed through my tears at his joke, smiled my trademark smile through the pain. My smile had changed but I was alive, and lucky.

I didn't speak of Jake in rehab, court ordered after the crash. I followed the rules of my NDA and focused on my mother, the stories other addicts shared, the assurances we all received that we were not alone the way we thought we were. We weren't to blame, therapists said, though I knew this was a lie. Still, I tried not to even think of Jake, and mostly I succeeded. Until I FaceTimed with Leah. It was her birthday. I remembered the day, texted, and we set a time to talk. I sat in the rehab "café," watched workers swap out trays of breakfast foods for the pudding cups and fruit cups and juice boxes offered between meals. Leah sat on the balcony of her studio apartment and seemed nervous when she answered. "We broke up," she said of her boyfriend. She hadn't cried about it, "Not once." So the gym plan was off. She was starting a new job soon, for an animal rights nonprofit. "You know, I've always been passionate about giving a voice to the voiceless," she said, her own voice ironed out like I was an interviewer. She told me about "initiatives," "campaigns across platforms." It all sounded clinical, like corporate porn, the sort of content Instagram turns up when you search for nudes: girls like I had been, girls Leah seemed to emulate after I posted her picture; girls in the shape of new characters for her to play. In the FaceTime box her lips were overlined, her foundation high definition and heavy. She'd taken the followers I'd given her, the followers her boyfriend had given her, and built them up. The number 16,000 sat beneath her handle now. "I thought I might get an even bigger platform with the gym," she said. "But you already know how that turned out." That's when Jake appeared in my mind, his pewter lenses peering over the top of an iPhone, then back at the screen, pinching to zoom in, fitting me inside the square, shooting. It was how I remembered him best.

Over FaceTime, Leah read me a poem her new boss had found on Pinterest and emailed to the office Listserv. "The tender-bellied wolf within rolls over to be loved," she began. Already, I thought the poem was bad. The writer was an Instagram sensation; celebrities often shared screenshots of her poems, often without attribution. Often, they were called out about it. "The wolf is beautiful whether or not people see the wolf/In every season, the wolf is the wolf," Leah read. "Be like the wolf." I watched her mouth move, listened to her voice. I could see my friend was sick, but also soft, trying to survive. I wanted to protect and help her. "I love it," I said when she was done.

I FOLLOW THE child's voice to the *Fairy Godmother's Magic Wand Shop Experience*. The line is long but moves quick. Those in front of me are processed and spit out to the gift shop where interactive wands and swords and slippers and scepters await, borderline reasonable at fifty-two bucks. Soon it will be my turn to shop, but for now I listen to a kid up front school his parents in curses, which are essential plot points in any fairy tale, he tells them. "It's usually True Love's Kiss that breaks the curse," the child says. "But sometimes it's more like crying, or an accident." The story gets me to the point in line where I can see the shop I'm aimed for, *Fairy Godmother's* traced in gold over paneled windowpanes. Behind the glass, props pile neatly. The mushrooms move further down inside me. I know it's dark inside the shop; I remember this part, can trust my memory of this one part, my mother and I, last ones in before the door shut. The crowd was thick in front of us and we stood on our tiptoes to see. But neither of us could, not well like we wanted.

Psychedelics are our teachers, another line of Jake's. What is the lesson in any of these stories: the prince, trapped in an animal's body; the sleeping girl, encased in glass. What is the lesson in True Love's Kiss and long wait times and crowds of sweating followers? 175,000 followers: the number where I landed before I left @annawrey behind. 175,000 may sound like a lot. But it's worth nearly nothing.

For years after my mother died, I gathered those followers, procedures, parties, and waited for her to return, send a sign, make me wise and womanly the way I told myself she had been. She had been the right kind of woman: chaste and maternal, natural and correct about the source of her own illness, a martyr when nobody believed her soon enough to save her life. But that's not who she was, not totally. And that's never who I'll be.

Still, I miss her. I don't know her. Not the way some women grow up and learn to know their moms. Sometimes, around my period mostly, I cry for us both, what she endured, what I have to live without. The sad fact that I'll never again be seen by her.

Once, I wandered down an internet rabbit hole, found a website for a product called True Mirror™, which claims to show you to yourself as others see you. Conventional mirrors flip the reflection and therefore aren't true, the website said. But the True Mirror™, built of several mirrors, shows you how you look in other people's eyes. *Mirror, mirror on the wall, who is the fairest of us all?* read a banner at the top of TrueMirror.com. *Have YOU been looking in the mirror your whole life and deluding yourself?* the rest of the sales pitch went. *Now, for only five hundred dollars, you can own the one True Mirror™ in which you can gaze and know, finally, how you appear to the world.* Amazon reviewers of the product expressed either shock, outrage, or enormous relief. "FINALLY, I KNOW THE TRUTH," said one I still remember. It almost convinced me to buy a True Mirror™ of my own. But the expense, and some small shred of wisdom stopped me. It's a scam. Every mirror is an illusion. The only one I want is the one my mother offered, a vision of myself through her eyes. For years now, I've lived in her cottage, our cottage, paying down the mortgage, refinancing to pay for Aesthetica™; waiting, on some unconscious plane, for her to come back and see me. But she isn't coming back. It's up to me to look upon myself the way I imagine she would: with love. Maybe that's the wisest approach to the life left for me to move through, age into. It's a privilege, to age, I see that now.

AFTER ME, BLAZE the brand grew, went Wall Street public, changed nothing when former Buds came forward with allegations of assault. Jake remained untouched and went on recruiting new versions of @annawrey until he quit six years ago, transformed into a survivalist, a husband, a dad. His last girlfriend before the rebrand was twenty-one with perfect natural breasts and, as I watched her following grow, longer lashes, a slimmer nose, larger lips and eyes turned up at the corners like a cat's. It appeared she also developed freckles, a small signifier of girlish imperfection. Permanent makeup artists were tattooing them to hot girls' cheeks, I read, a trend started by a successful indie movie actress with freckles that guys found both sexy *and* cute. But no matter how I zoomed, I could never confirm the change in Jake's girl's face. I wonder if *Vanity Fair* has contacted her. She's a verified wellness influencer now, with a patented facial massage technique and attendant products—rollers, microcurrents, oils—to draw out consumers' natural beauty, and take the place of toxins. She has a lot to lose, by going on the record. More than me, certainly.

In the years since I started selling makeup and skincare, I've thought a lot about people's real faces, the small intricacies that might someday go viral. Hook noses, close-set eyes, asymmetries of every sort. I've considered how Botox and filler might be used to accomplish ugliness. I've looked at my own face and thought the toxin, the acid, already worked this way. Before Aesthetica™, I was stuck in between times. I looked older than my age, but eerily wrinkle free, neither a girl nor a woman, and even if I wanted to express a feeling about it, I couldn't. I knew it was a problem, but still visited the med spa every three months like I was going to church. And every time I made the drive, I felt excited, like this treatment would be the treatment that changed everything. After, I was often so depressed I cried on the way home. It's the same when I go to see my drug dealer, a pattern. I understand the basic psychology of the pattern. But until now, I've followed it like a map.

NOW I'M NEXT in the *Fairy Godmother's* line. Now I am inside, knocking into shelves of props and other tourists' bodies. I'm stoned, I realize when they turn, give me guarded smiles. I watch their eyes flit from my knockoff shades to the hood of my sweatshirt and remember how I look. It doesn't matter. It's dark enough to hide myself, my awkward high, which suits the room, the magic mirrors climbing to the ceiling, the prosthetic pumpkins, poison apples, a stack of golden straw and a spindle, needle shining. Fairy Tale fans pack in behind me, some wearing costumes. More bodies squeeze in the back before the door shuts and takes with it the last piece of light.

Everyone knows to keep quiet now. Everyone knows the voice comes next. It begins, old and warm and belonging to a woman. "Bibbidi bobbidi boo, I'm your Fairy Godmother," the voice says. Fake candles turn up and lift the room around its edges. I feel my own attention, rapt like it belongs to someone else. I feel my skin, feel blood and guts and Aesthetica™. I breathe in and out, imagine my dirty air rising up, mixing with everyone else's.

The actor playing the Fairy Godmother appears from the shadows, wearing a white wig and purple cape, pink circles rouged onto her cheeks. She's authentic enough for me not to think about her real life, the sad apartment, ashtrays, bills, unrealized dreams. She scans the room, smiling. I stand up taller.

"You there," she says, and gestures at the front row. "Come forward, child." A boy of ten-ish steps from the crowd.

"I see you are a prince, are you not?" the Godmother says.

The child looks at his feet, nods.

"Good, good," the Godmother says and scans the shelves. "Now, let's see." She passes the kid a plastic sword. "Give it a wave," she says.

The boy holds it up, swings. Sound effects whiz and thunder.

"Certainly not," the Godmother says and grabs the sword back. "Never fear, sometimes it takes several tries."

The scepter she hands him next is also a dud and sets off a fake explosion.

"Wrong," she says and mimes contemplation.

The boy has his eyes on the actor now, like he's forgotten what's not real.

"HOW DO YOU see the world?" my rehab therapist asked the day I arrived and again the day I left. A pattern of tragedy, respite, tragedy, I said both times. But this wasn't always the case. "Be the wolf," Leah recited, and once I thought I could. Once I thought I could use power, the people who had it, the men, to make me immune to loss. I had the privileges attached to health and youth and whiteness. And a wide open something I mistook for beauty. I imagine it now as an invisible mark, an absence where a father went, a fear of who I'd be without a mother. She had always been sick, and even when I pushed her away, even as I tried to be different, I knew to fear her loss. I am responsible; I am not at fault. I want to feel that both are true. Here, in this replica, this room that is both present and past, I bargain with my brain, consider the worth of a story like mine. I am neither lost nor found, lucky nor cursed, and no fairy Godmother is coming to save me. From the bag strapped to my back I feel my phone, buzzing.

AT THE FRONT of the room, the Godmother paces. She stops, puts a finger to her cheek and taps. "Wait just a minute," she says and then, "no, it can't be," and then, "but maybe, just maybe." Awestruck music starts soft and builds.

The Godmother climbs the ladder, removes a long, white wand with a red, plastic heart on the tip.

"This special wand symbolizes True Love's Kiss," she says. "It has the power to break even the strongest curse." She places the wand in the child's outstretched hand. The soundtrack crescendos and the room goes pitch. A bright beam shines down on the boy only.

"True Love will guide you," the Godmother cries and all the lights come up.

I EXIT TO the gift shop. And that's when I see them, the woman and girl from the hotel pool, standing off to the side, bargaining. "Isabelle honey, that wand was a prop," the mother says. "We'll get you your own." Her forehead elevens are up and working.

Isabelle, the girl, is pouting too. "There's only one true love," she says, bossy like her mom should know that. I float closer, feel fluffy and spatially impaired, playing with a boring brown wand I wave too close to other people's bodies while I eavesdrop. Isabelle and her mom consider a silver scepter, but it's not original enough, Isabelle says. I listen to her hate every option her mom presents and flick my wand back and forth, in and out of thoughts I can't hold on to, most of them about myself. In my bag, my phone buzzes again and I put the wand back, remove my device, check the screen.

"How'd it go?" Leah has texted, presumably about Aesthetica™, possibly in response to the call I think I remember placing now, sometime last night. But it's all a blur and I'm embarrassed to admit it, or to tell her about Henry, or show her who I am, how I look now that it's only my real face I'm wearing. I swipe the text away, drop my phone back in my bag, watch Isabelle decide on a pretty magic wand with a star on the tip. Then I carry the goth wand I'm holding—a goofy skull on the hilt, mouth open, asymmetrical eyes—to the registers where I use the last of Henry's cash to buy it.

OUT IN THE alley, I keep my eyes pinned on the back of Isabelle's mom's red head, the clasp of her hand around her daughter's hand. I follow them to the first interactive hot-spot where lasered Fairy Tale props can work, a giant screen where twelve animated princesses have paused mid-dance, like the victims of a bad internet connection. They're supposed to start dancing again when an interactive device air-letters an *M* in front of the screen and I get in line, close where I can listen to Isabelle fret as every kid ahead of her struggles. Some of them give up.

"Maybe you have to be tall enough," she says and stands up straighter. Her mom takes out her phone to film.

"You've got this," the mom says. When her turn comes, Isabelle puts her feet where they're supposed to go and bends her knees like she's ready to take flight. She lifts her magic wand, makes a swish. But the princesses don't budge.

"Dang," she says and tries again, to nothing.

"One more time," her mother says. "Try it one more time."

"I can't," Isabelle says.

"One more try."

The girl stomps, then plants her feet. Even with her baby fat and freckles there is a maturity to her stance, a determination. Isabelle is not my child. I think this as I watch her lift her wand, close her eyes, draw an *M*. Slowly, the orchestra music rises, the girls begin to twirl.

"I did it!" Isabelle yells.

Not my child. But if she was, I would tell her to hold fast to her wand, her power. Not my child, but I can still act in the service of her future. I can share a story to help make the boundaries between reality and illusion easier for her to consider and choose.

"I did it!" Isabelle yells again.

"I knew you could," her mother says and we move on.

"I THINK I'M getting sicker," Leah said when I got out of rehab and we started talking again. "But I can't stop running." We texted and FaceTimed often after that. Still do. We talked while she contemplated treatment, quit, tried again. Talked while I hocked waist trainers, hair serums, laxative tea and considered rebrands I could try. Wellness, recovery, fitness, mother-loss, motherhood, all journeys I could start fresh. Or

I could throw my meager weight behind a cause, the dying oceans maybe. But stunned and scarred, I did nothing. Slowly, I stopped posting. My sponsors dropped me, some followers dropped me, though many of them remain, shackled to the ghost of a girl they thought they loved. "Classic @annawrey," they sometimes comment on the Hippy Baby pictures, the Vegas casino shots. "So pretty before she did her lips," they say, or talk about how the boob jobs and facial implants, the filler and fat grafting and butt injections ruined my body. I've tried to stop reading about what they think, what they miss, which @anna they loved. I go to work at the makeup counter in the black and white striped store, where the real women are.

"I'M SORRY I abandoned you," I've said to Leah more than once.

"You can stop apologizing now," she always says. I don't know if I ever can, don't know how much regret it'd take to return to what we had as girls. As it is, we've made a distant love out of a bond that seemed once like life itself. We're at home in each other's imperfect recovery, the imperfect pasts we forget, remember, live around like conditions no one deserves but eventually, almost certainly, contracts. This I know: the certainty of tragedy and respite; Leah's body across oceans and time. She is one beginning of my story. My mother is another. But there are more. Summer 2017, for example. Fifteen years ago. Some chain wax center in West Hollywood and my half-naked body reclined on a sheet of butcher paper. And every transformation that followed, every body I became. Up until now it's been that beginning I've clung to, the past, my girl-hood. But it's my future on the table now, a future reality that's mine to create. An old entrepreneurial script returns to me and I see that my story, which for so long I've kept silent, a source of shame, is the key to my next life, the rebrand I've been waiting for. Procedures are not the only measure of trans-formation. Nor is Instagram. But Aesthetica™ has worked. I am ready. I can speak. I can survive.

I've kept far enough behind Isabelle and her mom not to be an obvious tail. This is what I tell myself, though perhaps I'm wrong. We weave up and down the alley and I reach in my bag, remove my phone again, check the screen while I walk. The crowd has lifted, or I've surrendered to its press. I'm safe, if stifled, and the drugs I thought had failed make the phone I hold a mirror in which my own willingness to see failure stares back at me like a body I don't want. I look at my reflection. I try to count her angles. From one she is beautiful, from another she is stuck, wrong. Then time has passed and she's a spectrum. I select Leah's last text, watch the cursor, blinking. I move to my Instagram, open my messages, press the reporter's name. "I'm ready," I write, and send. I know where to begin.

ISABELLE AND HER mom stop for candy apples drip-ping with caramel "poison" and calories and I buy one too. We eat, wipe our faces, watch an enchanted pumpkin become a beautiful carriage, then a pumpkin again. We come to a window on a screen that opens with the correct incantation; we come to a secret passage in a wall that leads where? A dungeon, an escape, true love and womanhood. The child practices each spell until she gets it good enough. "Try again," her mother urges when she fails. Here, she traces the slope of a question mark; here, the shape of a heart. Here, at the end, she follows a pattern—swoop, lift, tap—to unlock the last door.

ACKNOWLEDGMENTS

Thank you to my agent, Erin Harris, for taking on this novel, going with me when I wanted to make it even weirder and then helping me fight for it. Thank you to Mark Doten, Alexa Wejko, Rachel Kowal, Bronwen Hruska and the whole team at Soho for the wonderful home; it's an honor to work with you. Thank you Allison Brainard.

Thank you Sarah McColl, Kimberly King Parsons, Chelsea Bieker, Cyrus Simonoff, T Kira Madden, Genevieve Hudson, Dantiel W. Moniz (BAWS forever), Nada Alic, Tea Hacic-Vlahovic, Raegan Bird, Michelle Gutes Guterman and *The Drunken Canal*, Asher Penn, Zach Sokol, and *Sex Magazine*, Ashley Wurzbacher, Sarah Gerard, Cristine Brache, Tao Lin, Caroline Calloway, Paige Woolen, Katie Adams, Diana Arterian, Elizabeth Hall, The Forever Girls: Madeline Cash and Anika Jade Levy, Sally Sum, Kahle Buse, Ariella Rojhani, LeeLee Bookwalter, Lara Phillips, Judy Rasmuson, George Rowbottom, Penelope Bodry-Sanders, Cecile Just, Richard Mogavero.

Special thank you to my therapist, Yelena Tokman, who helped me build something that is mine for keeps—this book exists thanks to our work.

And thank you, always and above all, to my love and inspiration, Jon Lindsey.